Lilacs out of
the Dead Land

Books by RACHEL BILLINGTON

All Things Nice

The Big Dipper

Lilacs out of the Dead Land

Lilacs out of the Dead Land

by

RACHEL BILLINGTON

Saturday Review Press · New York

To Kevin

Lilacs out of
the Dead Land

I

ENGLAND TO SICILY

'I had a cable from Emmie this morning,' said Lawrence in the taxi on our way to London airport. He had picked me up at the flat. I looked dubiously at our cases together on the floor. They were as disparate as ourselves: his khaki leather, well-travelled; mine red corduroy with plastic edgings and a zip. It was raining outside the windows. Lawrence took my hand which I felt was cold and grubby like some underground animal's. He laughed gaily:

'Emmie is crazy.' He pulled out the telegram from his pocket: 'Did I tell you earth quick produced palace to rumble. Living in Hotel Jolly. Much Jolly. Champagne waiting darlings.'

I almost managed a smile, though rather at the prospect of a hotel than at the mis-spellings. I had been terrified by the thought of Emmie and Enrico over their breakfast table; her in silk-sashed hostess gown with thonged sandals; him smoking a cheroot under a pair of dark glasses.

'Well, have you got a curtain ring ready?' Lawrence lifted my hand to his mouth and bit it gently. 'Or shall I pretend you're my daughter?'

We were taking one of the direct flights to Palermo. It was Tuesday night, late and black and I felt as if I was jumping off a cliff.

It was still night when we landed. Only a few lights lit

the tiny airstrip. 'Come here,' Lawrence held out a hand as we walked across the tarmac. I moved to him obediently and disappeared into his heavy arms. 'Stay close,' he whispered. He seemed to be as big and warm as the night itself which wrapped us round with the smell of coffee and sea. 'I want to feel we discover this land together.' My eyes stared vacantly past his shoulder and came to rest on the massive blocks of black mountains which enfolded the airport. 'This will be our island.' He kissed my forehead in tender consecration.

'I'm glad they haven't met us,' I said as we took our cases from a conveyorbelt set with total irrelevance in the middle of an empty room.

'They're probably drinking the champagne. It is hot in here.' Lawrence took off his jacket and he wore under it a blue shirt which was smooth-ironed and cool. I thought of his wife.

'I want you to burn a rich golden colour so that I alone can see where the white parts begin. Tomorrow we'll go to the sea.'

I tried to realize we were in a foreign country. But as usual when I was with Lawrence I could only see the circle of air surrounding him. There were other people in the airport, I knew, but they seemed very small. Which, as a matter of fact, they probably were. Certainly the car which the Avis man handed over to us with such pride cramped Lawrence's legs so that he looked like a stork in a nest.

'Why have you rented a car?' I asked.

'I thought we might *fare un giro*.' He put his face close to the windscreen and then, leaning back against his seat, half-turned to me: 'We can't stay locked in the Jolly Hotel for five days.' Which surprised me because I remem-

2

bered one night of love, a long-spun romance of a hotel bedroom—the only walk to the bathroom or balcony. He was so lazy, except when making love. The laziest man I knew. So heavy, so thick.

'I want us to have done something together,' he said. But I suspected some other reason. Perhaps, after all, he was afraid I would bore him. We had never been so long together. Yet since I was only the embodiment of his own romantic nature, to tire of me would be to tire of himself. And he loved himself. His sensuous self. It never aged.

I sat in the car with the window open and the only thoughts that came to me were of him, wrapping me round like the smoke wreathes a genie's lamp. One thousand and one nights of love.

2

ENGLAND

Steam rises around me in moist exhalations of heat. My body lies in the bath like a pattern of white stones on a river bed. I admire its smooth circles and ovals from above. The patch of black hair waves its tendrils like an underwater plant and my toes are two bunches of pink flowers. And my breasts ... I put out my hand to touch them. They float on the water like lilies with a dark bud at the centre. The dark bud tightens under my fingers.

My face I can only imagine. It is not round like my body. It is angular and secretive. The eyes looking down now through the steamy vapours are moss green, sunk behind the nose craggy like a beak and the cheek-bones red-patched and prominent. My mouth is very red and curls like the rim of a volcano above my narrow chin. My face is wild and not at all soft. Black hair springs out from it like a pine forest on the edge of a barren cliff. The black profusion finds sap in my head which my features hardly suggest. My body must find the same source.

The bathroom suits my body. It is opulent and smooth. A wide low room without windows which feels as if it is underground. The bath is sunk in the floor which is covered with thick mushroom-coloured fur. Sometimes I think as I lie here that I will sink further and further down until I disappear altogether in the centre of the earth. There are no walls near and the door is behind me. The ceiling is marbled with mauve and blue and grey and if I look up I think I am seeing skin where the veins trace an incomplete pattern. It is very warm.

The bathroom in Lawrence's house was as large and luxurious as the bedroom.

My body lay submerged in the water, like my mind, blown with food, wine, and exhaustion. A painted puppet with the strings laid down. Black prickles poked uncomfortably along the white legs like hair still growing on a mortuary corpse. The steam rose round me in sickening wet circles but the cold-water tap seemed as remote from my lifeless hand as rain in the sky.

Lawrence would not enjoy a hot sweating corpse with a razor in its hand. But he hated it if I opened windows and at his age he should know women grow hair on their legs.

It was certainly harder to be a mistress than a wife. I sighed.

I often sighed; not a shallow cynical sigh but a deep slow heave which sometimes turned into a yawn. It did this time. I had an excuse—it was late, after dinner. But I didn't have an excuse because it was one of my few evening-stretching-into-night-to-breakfasts with Lawrence. His wife was away. We had been out to a fashionably well-attended restaurant in which Lawrence feared and hoped to be recognized.

We had each drunk two whiskies, a bottle of wine and a glass of Napoleon brandy—this despite Lawrence's notoriously delicate stomach. The brandy was due to the disappointment of not being recognized or, perhaps, to fortify himself against the long sleepless night ahead. We both felt a guilty duty to stay awake on our Golden Nights of Love.

I lay in the bath with my eyes closed.

'How beautiful you look.'

He had come in silently. I rearranged my limbs more elegantly. My body was round and curved and looked better arranged elegantly. Lawrence admired its classical lines. His wife was thin and hardly physical at all. Lawrence used to say I never looked *nude* nude and that he liked me better undressed than dressed. He also liked to wander round naked himself since his wife wouldn't let him. It made me feel very uneasy. Sexy and uneasy.

'So beautiful.'

I opened my eyes; I could never really believe in him. He was so handsome, so distinguished. He was everything you could want in a father. So tall, brown-skinned, gently commanding—I felt all these things about him to the point of veneration. I never overcame a sense of sacrilege when he took off his clothes or when he kissed me.

That night the drink had made him adventurous. He took off his white towel and strode into the bath. The water rushed up round us as his weight settled upon me. He had beautiful skin; thick and smooth with just two moles across the shoulder blades. I used to put a finger on each and press them as if they were control buttons. But that night in the bath my body was hot and the brandy was spinning in my head.

'My goddess . . .'

It was early in the night to have finished making love. Although the spirit would probably move us again towards dawn.

Lawrence lifted himself clumsily off me. The water drained down the side of the bath till I was left with

6

barely a trickle to cover my bottom. I felt as drained as the bath. My hair lay in wet black tangles on my shoulders. I could imagine the pain as I tried to comb it.

'Bed.'

I put out my arm and the fingers dangled helplessly over the shiny ledge. Lawrence had gone for a shower; his movements were made more precise by making love while mine were made vaguer.

'Bed.'

He came back rubbing his head vigorously with a towel. He had a lot of thick greyish-yellow hair. He pulled me out of the bath and propelled me towards the shower with a proprietary tap on my behind. He would never have done that before we made love. I hated him doing it any time. My resentment carried me through the shower and rubbed me dry.

Lawrence had gone to bed; he liked to lie there and wait for me. He said when you got older, waiting for something nice was the best part of life.

The bedroom was dark but I left the light on in the corridor as we liked a glow over our lovers' whisperings. Besides, in complete darkness, one of us might have fallen asleep.

'I dreamt I was in the country when we made love. In a golden field of corn sprinkled with scarlet poppies and dark blue cornflowers. Persephone. My Persephone. My goddess.'

What could I say? How does a goddess reply? I wanted my pedestal. I didn't want my pedestal. I lay in his arms while he surrounded me with romance. And we were both surrounded with the smell of saffron soap which his wife had chosen.

7

'It's so black,' I whispered. The anonymous statement of a goddess.

But it did seem blacker than usual as if we had sunk further away from the world. I said this to him and he loved it.

'Where have we fallen together? What black abyss have you found? While I was smelling sweet flowers in the sun, where were you, my black queen of night? What wild dreams fill your narrow head? Are you older than I am? Or have you lived before?'

Again I was silenced. I used to try to float with him, but now instead I looked for diversions. He was breathing noisily through his nose.

'Music. I'd love to hear music.' I put out a hand and stroked his cheek. He was lazy now; I was energetic.

'Sweet music, my darling.' He laid his hand on my shoulder and then my back as I slid out of bed. It transmitted vibrations of his satisfaction. He let it fall contentedly from me onto the bed.

I went downstairs to the drawing-room. Lawrence's stereo system was a lover's perk I enjoyed fully. Although it was controlled downstairs there were two speakers on either side of the bed—an idea which I had convinced myself was his, not his wife's. I sat my bare skin on the thick rug and surrounded myself with his records. I decided to impress him with a Bach suite for solo 'cello. The music made the whole room vibrate. I looked at my face in one panel of the three-panel mirror over the Regency London fireplace and the image shivered and seemed to move.

3

SICILY

'Look, isn't that "Jolly"?'

I started guiltily at Lawrence's voice, screwing up my eyes in a concentrated effort to prove I hadn't been falling asleep.

'I can't exactly...' We were travelling on a wide road beside the sea; to our right the city of Palermo loomed massively inward. 'Where've they hidden the indicator?'

I peered unhelpfully forward. 'Hotel Jolly. Good.'

At first I thought Lawrence was referring to a tasteful, pink-washed villa with green shutters shining in the artificial light.

'Are you tired, my dove?'

'Oh, no!' And then, as we swept right, I saw the great modern building with fierce jutting balconies.

Lawrence stalled the car at a rakish angle in front of it and got out.

'Better to be inside the ugly one.' He looked up at the entrance hall. And there was a hairpin figure backlit by the lights of the foyer and waving a bottle. '*Evviva!*' it cried and immediately a scurry of little dark figures ran out from either side of her and poured down the steps towards us.

'One thing Emmie always commands is service,' said Lawrence indulgently. 'My darling, we have arrived.' And then she was on us with the champagne bottle triumphantly aloft:

9

'I knew you'd be tired,' she hugged Lawrence. 'So this is for you. We are going to the only party in Palermo for six years—since my wedding party as a matter of fact—and you are to join us there. Enrico is infuriated because I was two hours changing, so he is already gone.' And then she was too. In a Mercedes with an aerial as high as a steeple.

'I always suspect Emmie of having dealings with the Mafia,' said Lawrence.

When we found our room, before I could rub my hot feet against the smooth-tiled floor or pull off my clothes to stand under the cooling shower, I found myself spread-eagled on the coverlet with Lawrence on top of me.

'My darling ... the whole journey ... so long ... I could feel you sitting beside me ... quiet, alone, remote from me ...'

The champagne rolled off the bed and dropped heavily to the floor. I felt myself submerged.

My skin seemed to flap against my bones as if a vampire had sucked off the vital blood. Lawrence was crouching by the bed trying to retrieve the champagne bottle. His hair stood on end and his skin was rather red and blotchy but his eyes were brilliant and triumphant. I lay back weakly.

'Tooth mugs, I think.' He was like a schoolboy at a midnight feast. The bottle top exploded against the wall and then against the ceiling then fell to the floor.

'Drink to Sicily,' he said, straddling my dead body and putting the cup to my lips. 'And then on to the celebration.'

I believe my passivity gave him his only moment of energy. So he loved it.

The champagne poured into my empty bloodless veins

so that I could feel the tingle even to my knees. I wondered how Emmie had guessed so exactly what I would need. She had left a route map to the party on the dressing-table. I put on a silk dress and sandals. It had little creases all down the front like a frown.

We drove along a black and vacant street cutting sharply through Palermo's heavy yellow buildings, now dark. My head fell forward.

'My darling!' Far away a hand touched my hair.

'It's the heat, I'm not used ... to heat in the evenings...' I thought it was my father's hand. But my eyes had closed as tight as mussels so I couldn't make certain.

I was woken by a sharp continuous noise like a thousand mechanical pecking birds. It shrilled through my head till eventually my lids clicked open. I saw around me a huge marble gallery filled with half-seen figures whose giant shadows cast up to the domed ceiling and whose voices, ejecting in disconnected echoes from their bodies, had woken me. I stared. Candles, caught in niches along the high walls, made jumping tiers of light.

'Are we in church?' I murmured. But then I saw we were moving towards a deep window which stretched out to a balcony. And a faint wind blowing in across my face seemed to clear my eyes.

We had arrived at the party.

The faces round the walls were colourful after all; not shadowy. Red lips, black-drawn eyebrows and skin as brown and rich as conkers. The men's heads, oval-shaped, set stiffly above their white silk polo necks, looked more like oil on canvas, formal portraits from a panelled dining-room than human flesh. True, their mouths moved, issuing the hard sounds I had heard first, but they opened and shut in such a rigid, flapping, clacking way, that it seemed a purely artificial performance. We reached the balcony and the night air appeared inexplicably bright till I noticed the stars overhead. They shone on several hills, almost mountains arranged in tiers around us, and on grey vineyards nearer to us and on the faces immediately around me.

I realized that the smooth hardness of lips and eyes, the sharp chins, the lacquered hair, the covered necks, were all a disguise. It was to disguise their age. They were old. I could feel myself standing young and soft between them like a white rubber ball amongst rocks.

Something touched my hand. And I turned to a sagging sharp long-nosed face which said:

'Monreale is behind us.'

We couldn't see behind us because of the house—or more exactly the castle—whose grey turrets and arched windows blocked our view.

'They're old!' I said accusingly, but Lawrence, young eyes become dead, brown skin become grey in the faraway light of the stars, blinked answeringly. Ashamed, I looked away and the hard incomprehensible hubbub struck my ears again. 'And they're all speaking Italian!'

Lawrence reached past me. He took a glass from a waiter's silver tray and curled it into my closed fingers.

'Drink is a universal language.' I watched as his thin dark strip of mouth stretched like a piece of elastic across his face. I emptied my glass and accepted another.

'The Tower of Babel,' I said, gripped all at once by the conviction I slept and this was a nightmare. But the figures didn't disappear with this knowledge. On the contrary, they seemed to grow brighter all the time. And the noise became louder. Till behind us in the room a woman peremptorily clapped her hands. I knew it was a woman because of the quickness and high-pitched speed of it and the additional sound of jangling bracelets.

Obediently like silly waves following the moon we drew round to where she stood. I wondered where Emmie was, for this woman was like her—with long thin arms bound in bracelets and hinged to the top of her shoulders with a little round button of bone. Except her hair was ebony black. In one hand she held a candelabra. Setting this on the floor between her feet, she began to roll off her bracelets. Each one separately with perfect concentration. And as she did so someone near began to clap. And then someone more. Till all around me ringed hands, manicured hands, smooth brown hands, male and female, were beating in unison. I noticed with a sense of my own foreignness how they used the base of their palms instead of their whole hands as the English do and then I, too, joined the drumming pulse. The fingers and faces disappeared behind the noise and only the woman in the centre of the room remained.

Slowly, one by one, she took off her bracelets, letting each drop as it came free and fall to the marble floor with a metallic clang. It punctuated our beat. When she had stripped off every bracelet she touched her neck with her hand still ornamented with rings and then, pushing her head back so that her neck was exposed long and golden in the candlelight. It seemed like the road to her body. From it she unclasped three necklaces, now stretching convulsively, now crouching to lay them lovingly at her feet. She stood, rising from her jewels, dressed in flowing folds of silk which swished gently with the wind blown in from the mountains. As the flames of the candle below her rose and fell she was like an Indian widow on her funeral pyre. Now, gracefully, as if to my Indian thought, she curled down to the ground fakir-like, and sat cross-legged. Slowly she unwound each foot from the gold-thonged sandals, twisted up her legs and then in a sudden movement stood up again, throwing out across the room little pointed jewels hidden in the folds of her dress, red glowing studs from her ears and the rings from her fingers. They fell like drops of rain around her. Till only her hair, wound long and dark with embroidered ribbons, glittered still.

Then we began to beat louder and I felt the floor vibrate as feet moved in unprogressing march upon it. My arm was taken on one side and then on the other; we were all part of a flowing circle.

Now in front of us she was rippling up and down, her golden yellow, green-streaked wrappings as much part of her as the silky arms and legs which floated in and out of them. Gradually, like snakes' tongues, her limbs coiled out further and further, and I saw sliding across the floor silken pieces of cloth—discarded but unwilling to die. A piece clung round my ankle and I let it stay.

Shiny supple limbs and a face masked; eyes shut, mouth half-open. My ears were already filled with our own noise and I saw rather than heard a hissing start from her tongue and slip through her mouth.

It grew and grew till the room was rippling, sizzling with it like ripe barley in a wind. The clapping, beating, stamping died away and we were suspended on this tide of hissing. Louder and louder. It grew. Louder and louder. Till it stopped. The sea ran back from the shore and the golden brown pure animal body clean and naked twisted itself backwards in wide-open defiance of us all. At that moment in the silence there was a gentle swish and her hair trailing from her abandoned head slipped from her

14

forehead and fell in a smooth mass to the floor. Short blonde hair stood up in wet prickles round her scalp.

I looked for a reaction; looked round. But the painted faces were blank and staring; open-mouthed; a few moved, touching each other with their hands but their faces were blank and staring.

Fingers touched my ribs pushing me unresisting round till I was pressed quite close to Lawrence's face as blank and stiff as all the rest. But I was still seeing the black hair fall to the ground which seemed to happen a thousand times over and over as if it would never stop. Till the pale prickles were revealed again. I stared, eyes wide and straining in the flickering light. Then I wanted to laugh. It was such a funny sight! I took a step forward.

The front prickles of hair were starting to bend as the weight of the water rolled down slowly towards the tip where it gathered into a large drop. It hung there for a moment suspended; until all at once the hair dipped in a little bow and like a great pearly tear it slipped away. After all it was not funny.

'It's not funny,' I said and felt my eyes swelling. 'It's not funny; it's terribly, terribly sad.' And I pressed myself insistently forward like an animal nuzzling its mother.

4

ENGLAND

My father welcomes me home Christ-like with his arms held wide. His beard is black and neat. I hug him and his tweed coat smells of the countryside.

'A long time since we saw you here,' he says, and the gruff words string out along the sunbeams through to the darker hall. It is morning and the house is being stroked and smoothed for a new day.

'Hello!' I say to Flossie, who stops the Hoover for a minute.

'You chose a lovely morning, miss.'

I have come from another world. My limbs are hidden, clothed in shiny magazines, I have come from London; come from my lover.

'Your mother's in her room.'

My mother is upstairs wavering in the pattern of her flower-printed wallpaper.

'Darling, what a surprise!' curved hands raised in a froth of white soap. One bubble breaks and a drop of water falls glistening to the carpet. Through the open window the birds sing.

'Look how your rose has clambered up,' I say and lean out of the window.

'Be careful you don't fall,' says my mother. 'How long are you staying?'

The daughter returns home. I go along to my room and touch with love the china horse and the picture I won in

16

a raffle and the books I bought with the first money I
earned and the bed ... my own bed.

My face fits to the pillow and my toes curl over the
end. I know where my dolls are wrapped in plastic and
love. I know where my old clothes lie with lavender
sachets.

And outside the view; wide green-shading trees. The
old swing on the great oak tree, the pink-tiled shed that
was my house as a child. The fields that I ran in and rode
in and loved. I fling off my clothes and throw open the
window. I am home. I am home.

I arrived home, in Dorset, earlier than I usually woke
up on a Saturday. At the front door, I met my father,
ruddy and energetic, on his way to golf. Though surprised to see me and no doubt ready to be pleased he
had no intention of delaying his much-looked-forward-to,
hallowed-by-time, once-weekly game.

'A long time since we saw you here,' he said offering
the quick paternal peck which produced in me the usual
contradictions resolving into petty irritation.

I went inside quickly. The dark womb with cavernous
vibrations as Flossie twisted herself into the Hoover cord.
She looked up, stopped the machine. She seemed pleased at
any rate.

'You chose a lovely morning, miss.'

I didn't choose it. Lawrence's wife chose it. She woke
us up with the telephone at eight-thirty. She was coming
back with her child—I didn't want to know the reason.
We had fallen asleep at six. Lawrence was dull and stupid.
I leapt out of bed. She was only in Richmond. I felt her

17

approach already. Her and her child. The flat changed colour and became grey and ugly. Lawrence aged twenty years making him sixty. I decided to catch the train home.

'Your mother's in her room.' Flossie had a hierarchical view of things—mothers first. Obediently I went upstairs.

She was washing her pale lacey underclothes which she would hang out in the sunny garden. I thought of my own drawer full of dirty underclothes and immediately felt inferior and resentful.

'Darling, what a surprise!'

Please don't say who's coming to dinner, I prayed, wanting her for a moment to myself.

'Look how your rose has clambered up.' I diverted her flatteringly.

'Be careful you don't fall. How long are you staying? We've got the Brooks coming to dinner and a couple you don't know ... I wonder if we can find someone for you ...'

I shut my ears and went to my bedroom. The last retreat. An aphorism for defeat. The old things I tried to put behind me creeping up in moments of failure. Even the garden and countryside were a well-charted map of memories.

I turned away from the window. Had Lawrence taken my flight to heart? Most probably he was having a quiet elevenses with his wife and son. At least I had escaped him. I turned my back to the window, threw it wide open and tugging at my clothes with ungainly hands took them off my body. My grey petticoat in particular filled me with horror. I was sure it smelt of Lawrence. I flung it out of the window, but having no weight, it caught on a creeper and hung wispily still in my view. And there was a cool wind which made my skin goose-pimple. I tried to become glorious and free with my eyes shut to the air, but it was heavy air thick with the smells of home. So I gave up and went along to the bathroom.

I made the bath last till lunchtime. I was physically very clean when my mother and I met across the dining-room table. My hair was still wet.

'Be careful you don't catch a cold with your hair dripping down your back.'

'I'm tough.'

'I know, dear, but look what happened to Anna.'

I smiled and then sighed. Anna was my elder sister who had had a bad bout of pneumonia when a child.

'Anna was delicate. No one could describe me as delicate.' It was a family tradition. Also Anna was beautiful. Anna was good. This was not a tradition. This was true. There must be a basis for home life and in our family's case it was love of Anna.

'Of course not, dear. You've always had a lovely healthy figure. It's because you lived such an open-air life as a child. I hope you get enough exercise in London.'

'I walk to school, mother.' I also make love, mother, which is guaranteed to exercise every part of your body.

'Anna was a war baby.'

For some reason I never felt jealous of Anna.

'Yes, mother. The garden looks nice.' Perhaps it was because she was ten years older than me—so very far out of my reach.

After lunch we walked round the garden together. That also was a family tradition. I was supposed to like outdoor activities. I was also good-natured, reasonably pretty and adequately endowed with brains. I had never given my parents cause for worry in mind or body.

19

'I'd love to clip the hedge,' I said good-naturedly.

'You are a darling. I wish you'd come home more often.'

'Yes, mother.' I took the shears and a large pair of gardening gloves. 'And afterwards I'll walk round the fields.'

'That's right. While you've got the opportunity.' My mother tripped happily back to the house.

I wore an old school shirt and jeans. She would look out of her window and think I was still fifteen. The sun was hot on my forearms, the shears were heavy. I determined to finish the hedge. The dark green box leaves fell round my feet. The smooth-cut top was hard and unappealing.

'Well done!' cried my mother, happening to look out of her window as I finished.

Then I went for my walk. It was September and I could feel the days beginning to grow shorter. It was cool under the trees and the wind had become stronger. I felt very tired and my legs needed all the willpower my brain could provide to make them move. It seemed to me I was carrying an enormous load and as I crossed the seventh and last field on the route home, I identified that load as Lawrence.

Dinner that night was slightly worse than I expected. For one thing I had brought no luggage so I hopefully squeezed myself into an old dress I found in my cupboard. I substituted a red scarf for the too short belt and admired the negligent gipsy effect.

'Oh!' said my father as I came into the drawing-room. 'You've not got much time to change, you know.'

'I'm afraid this is all I've got,' I apologized humbly. And the doorbell rang, diverting my father.

'I hope we're not early.'

'No, of course not.'

'The Brooks are coming and...' My father ushered his guests into the drawing-room. 'You know Anna, but I don't think you've met my younger daughter, April. Jane and George Hatter.'

'How do you do?' The gipsy smiled and seemed about to curtsy. 'It's fun meeting someone new.' The gipsy stood awkwardly and stuck out her hand, but they were country people, uncritically happy on a social occasion.

My father went to answer the doorbell again.

'You're the teacher, aren't you?' Jane Hatter was nice. She wore a gay emerald-green dress with a brooch attached to her bosom. I wondered how long it took her to choose the perfect position—or did it sit there from social occasion to social occasion? George eyed the drinks table.

Mother likes to make an entrance. She swept in with the Brooks and father and a splendid bowl of cheese dip.

'Splendid!' cried George over his whisky. George was not unlike Lawrence to look at.

Luckily they hadn't found another man for me.

Half-way through dinner I started to feel sick. I longed for a book and bed.

My father came in and found me there when the guests had gone.

'I'm sorry, father. London's so tiring.'

'Of course. Of course.' His breath smelt of whisky. 'Mother was a little worried, that's all.'

I pulled up the sheets to hide my lack of nightdress which was the sort of disregard for convention which upset him.

'Work going all right?'

'Yes, thank you.' He sat on the bed which only emphasized the gulf between us.

'Jenny well?' He found the question with a smile. I shared a flat with Jenny and she had made a great impression on him. He always asked after her. The sound of her name made the birds sing. I think he hoped that I was like Jenny when he wasn't there—not that I wasn't a perfect daughter.

'She's got engaged.'

'Nice chap?'

'Very. He works in the city somewhere.' Jenny worked in publishing. Lawrence was the managing director of her firm.

We had met at a publisher's party to which Jenny had taken me. She said writers were the gayest company because they were so guiltily excited at the escape from their typewriters. Jenny thought I was too intense and intellectual. I cried a lot in the flat in London.

'What?' I said to my father who had turned at the door with an expectant face.

'I said Anna's definitely going to Australia. Almost at once.'

'Oh,' I murmured. 'How terribly sad.'

5

SICILY

Something was tickling my armpit. Perhaps a little snake or a piece of thread or even a delicate finger. Or perhaps I was lying on the grass outside my bedroom window in Dorset where the lavender burst over the flower bed and a flyaway shoot had caught in my dress. I felt very hot. But then it must be a gorgeous hot day to be lying on the lawn just there in such an unsheltered spot. On the other hand, I never did lie just there because too many people passed by on their way to the kitchen and my mother always had some suggestion for an occupation and moreover Anna often left the children there in the pram and they mustn't be disturbed. It must be a fly tickling me.

I opened my eyes but the blackness was as deep as before. It gave me no clue. However, putting my hand to my armpit, I discovered it was wet and tracing the wetness upwards found it started in the roots of my hair and trickled down my back round my shoulder into my armpit. Where it had woken me up.

Now I knew where I was. I felt my way across the room and opened a shutter. Lawrence's uncovered limbs displayed themselves in the other bed like a new statue from which the disguising sheet had just been swept aside.

I picked up a towel from the floor and began to rub my damp neck. Looking down through my nightdress to my body I saw with disgust my own pallid skin. A strip of sun where I had opened the shutters lay across the tiles. Rolling off my nightdress, I lay down within its warm boundary. Gradually the sun dried the sweat from the night before. Now I was able to recall the dead faces of yesterday with nothing but disbelief. Was the woman who danced Emmie? I admired my dispassionate curiosity. Had I simply fallen asleep at the end?

'Just like a cat!' Lawrence stood over me in a white bathrobe. His face seemed already darkened by the sun. He crouched down and stroked my hip. 'Not furry at all.' He was laughing.

'Was that Emmie last night?' I was lazy, half-asleep again.

'Oh! Emmie. Well, we did see her!' He was mysterious but I was too warmed to care. He pulled me up till I sat straight-backed facing him and then lay the palm of his hand flat across my chest above the breasts. 'While I talk with Enrico you must go to the beach and become a lovely golden.'

His commanding pleased me. I jumped up self-consciously graceful under his staring looks.

'And now I'll order breakfast.' He laughed again; indulgently; greedily.

We sat on the balcony in the thickening morning sun. It was already high above the sea, flaring golden in the sky. The sea was separated from us by a wide road roaring noisily with cars and lorries and motor bikes.

We sat on our little balcony gulping coffee. On either side of us more balconies, divided by frosted glass, enjoyed their own blinkered vision.

But the glass was not soundproof.

'Eleven a.m., Carey, and we've done Monreale and had a swim. Pretty fair. Now Segesta, Selinunte, Agrigento.'

24

The drawling American voice increased in volume. Two misshapen frosted figures appeared on the balcony to our left. Bunched skirts, bent heads. With jealousy I sensed their purpose and energy—in every gather of their skirts, in their loud voices, in the solid way their legs disappeared to the bottom of the glass. Lawrence apparently had not noticed them; he buttered a roll with immense satisfaction. He spread it with jam. He laid it deliberately into his mouth and chewed.

'I'd love to see something of Sicily while we're here,' I said and swung my leg over the side of the chair.

'Eager little body, aren't you, my darling?'

'Not really,' I said with an obstinate look. It wasn't noticed. He sat back happily with his coffee cup.

'I told you I'm planning to make a wee tour. Business first with Enrico and then pleasure.' He leant forward and took my hand which I was dangling impatiently. 'I love you when you're childish.'

'Childlike.' I got up and went in. But almost immediately, full of repentance, full of nervous dread, came out again. Lawrence hadn't moved.

'Hello, my darling,' he said, touching my thigh. 'Had a shower, have you?' His content had not been disturbed; his face was reddening from the sun. 'I suppose I'd better dress.' He heaved himself up regretfully.

I followed him indecisively to the bedroom.

'We haven't seen much of your friends,' I said.

'Emmie never gets up before lunch.'

With surprise I watched Lawrence put on pale corded trousers and a blue towelling sweater. Before he had only worn publisher's suits. Trousers and sweater were faded from other suns. I wondered where else, who else.

'I'll drop you off at the beach,' he said.

There was a turntable of postcards on the desk in the foyer. I twisted it vacantly and then took out three anonymously brilliant pictures of sea and sky.

'So, you're a postcard girl as well as a tourist.' Lawrence turned back to me from a long Italian conversation with the man at the desk. I looked at him again; he was much too elegant to be a clerk.

'I didn't know you spoke Italian.'

'Not very well any more. I lived in Rome as a child.'

I knew nothing whatever about him.

'Do you never send postcards?' We were in the car silently side by side and the silence was a barrier between us.

'Not when I've got with me the only person I want.' He pulled my knees nearer to his and I felt quite gay again. His approval set me free to look at the sea running on the right of us, to smell its rich saltiness and revel in the sun beating through the windscreen onto my knees. The postcards lay in my lap. But now I questioned the instinct that had made me buy them. Lawrence was right. They were a mockery of our freedom. All sharpened and lacquered for easy viewing. I threw them out of the window. Mother, father, Jenny and John. Instead I gave Lawrence a triumphant hug, which made him wobble the steering-wheel and smile cosily. 'It's so lovely to be here with you alone!' I cried. 'We could do anything!' After all, I thought, as I rested my head comfortably on his shoulder, was there anyone left in England now who merited a ready-reckoner to our brave new world? Or even wanted it?

6

ENGLAND

*Anna is dark. Anna is pale. Anna is smiling down at me
who bends to fasten the buckle of her shoe. Tonight she
is going dancing and I, who am only small, still a child,
can help her dress and watch her lovingly until she dis-
appears.*

*Anna is kind. Anna is good. In the daytime she wears
belts that fit round her waist like a watch-strap on a wrist.
She is loved by us all. And now she is loved by a man. He
is tall and broad in tail coats. I am dressed all in white
hovering like a snow flake round the snow queen for today Anna is married.*

*Anna has a husband, a house, two children. When I go
to Anna the best of me comes from behind my skin like
a silver lining and anything is possible.*

A visit to Anna's house was like taking the waters. I
approached it as to a cooling draught of happy memories.

One day at home and I was fed up. I could feel myself
sliding down the slippery slope to daughterly subser-
vience. Already at breakfast on Sunday morning I ate
four sausages because I was supposed to like four sausages, though I certainly don't. And then, of course,
church. I had to leave after that. My mother actually held
my hand as we left and my father became absurdly

knowing. So I said I had some exercise books to correct which I had foolishly left in London and such was their unquestioning confidence in me that they believed it and kissed a calm goodbye.

I didn't say I was going to Anna's on my way because I didn't like to mix my love with theirs.

'Don't leave it so long next time, darling,' said my mother.

'And give my love to Jenny,' said my father.

'Yes, father. Goodbye, mother. Do come and see me if you're in London. And of course father knows he always can ...' Father worked in the city three days a week. He had never invited me to his office.

Anna and her husband Gerry and their two sons Christopher and Timothy lived in a Victorian house on the outskirts of London. It was typical of Anna that she preferred to create her own world in a large, beautifully hideous, high-ceilinged, unheated, many-staired and storeyed house, backed by an impossible rambling garden, containing a home-constructed climbing-frame and a wooden veranda. The fact that it was irrevocably placed in an unfashionable and ugly modern suburb, with rows of plastic houses and yards of empty grey concrete, meant nothing to her. She was surprised that anyone thought her odd in wanting this rather than the claustrophobic alternatives in London. It never crossed her mind that she might become isolated. And already, because everything she did seemed the right thing to do, several of her friends were looking for houses in the area. And now, of course, she was leaving.

'The working girl herself!' Anna welcomed me happily, who should have been harassed—Sunday joint half out of the oven, children dropping knives in the dining-room.

'Here, let me help.' I came right into the kitchen.

'What timing!' she exclaimed with perfect acceptance as I took a skewer from between her teeth. As if she was expecting me.

'I hope you don't mind...'

'My dear April ... Grab a plate for yourself, would you?'

I watched her carry through the joint, admiring the casual way her coiled black hair clung to the back of her head, the way her scarlet Scholl sandals flapped securely against her bare pink heels, the way her flowered skirt gathered bouncily at the waist.

I picked up a large bowl of baked potatoes to follow her but decided first to cross the high white hallway to the living-room. One whole wall was covered by a gigantic cork notice board cloaked in a patchwork of newspaper clippings, scrawled notes, drawings by the children, photographs, bits of material and even dried flowers. I liked to check up on it every visit. This time I noticed immediately a new photograph of me with the children. I was wearing a smock and roaring with laughter. It was a very unromantic photograph. I turned away.

I placed the bowl of potatoes carefully on the dining-room table. It was dominated by a gigantic vaseful of dahlias.

'What glorious flowers!' I had never seen so many shades of orange and gold before. It made my head swirl, like looking at a kaleidoscope in the middle of the table.

'Christopher manures them daily, in person,' leered Timothy the older boy.

'The wind will change! The wind will change!' chanted Christopher with an even more evil leer. 'Anyway, I don't. I put dried blood on them.'

'The wind will change! The wind will change!' shrieked Timothy.

'Hi, April,' said Gerry, picking up the carving knife and running the blade up and down the sharpener, then standing back to better estimate the joint. He wore a hand-knitted green jersey and his hair stood partly on end. He had to be a lesser creature, Gerry, to me at any rate. Whenever possible, we talked football—at least I listened while he eagerly explained his team's four-three-four formation and their hopes for promotion which seemed to depend on half of England going down with smallpox and the other half being buried under snow. The boys would chew their nails with concentration while I nodded sagely.

'I hope it's not underdone,' Anna peered anxiously with a terrible frown between her eyes, below pale forehead, between wide eyes. As if the state of the meat was her biggest problem in life.

'If it is,' Timothy meditated with a faraway look in his eyes, 'we could use the live blood on the dahlias. All hot and steaming.'

'Silence, boys! Not at lunch, please.' Gerry ran the flashing sharp knife through the lamb and it was perfectly cooked.

'Oh good!' exclaimed Anna with enormous relief.

She possessed so exactly the secret of living for the moment. Her actions were a direct reflection of what she was thinking. And her thoughts followed logically one from the other so that I could trace Anna back to my early memories of her without a break or a worry. I always thought that if I stayed near her long enough, one day all my pieces would fit together and mirror her smooth front. Did she ever notice, I wonder, my slave-dog eyes?

'More meat, April?' said Gerry.

'Oh, thanks; it's so good.' It was obviously not the season for football, but I found it difficult to think of any better approach to him. I never had been successful in drawing him out on cricket. Perhaps he didn't like the game.

So eventually I exclaimed—loudly, to cover my emotion, 'Are you really going away then?'

An immediate current of electricity galvanized the table. Gerry raised his knife like an executioner and Anna hissed, with her finger to her mouth and her eyes rolled towards the children: *'Pas devant! Ils ne saient encore.'*

'Oh, I'm sorry ... I ...'

'What aren't we supposed to know?' mouthed Christopher through his baked potato.

'Don't speak with your mouth full,' said Gerry.

'There's treacle tart for seconds,' said Anna.

I stared guiltily past her head and tried to restore my composure by calmly surveying the thick white curtains with their rich embroidered trimming. I remembered very well when the trimming had edged one of her evening dresses.

After lunch the women did the washing-up. The men disappeared into the garden. Anna and I stood side by side at the sink.

'I'm sorry about all the drama,' she said, handing me a drying-up cloth in the shape of a heart. 'You see, we're not letting them know about Australia till the last minute—after Gerry's gone. He goes Wednesday and we follow on Friday. They'd be too dreadfully excited otherwise. Make our life murder.' She had a long-handled mop which

31

she was hauling in and out of the glasses with obvious enjoyment.

'Isn't it awful to leave your house, everything?'

'Oh, it is! But I was getting too much the proud house-keeper. Look, I'd actually started drawing pictures on the back of my scrubbing brush.'

I laughed. She really had, in bright oil paints, a picture of a dog, a cat, and a bear looking at each other.

'It's beautiful. Really.'

I never told Anna about Lawrence. I didn't want to sully her image with my own stupidities. Besides, as long as she didn't know I could expect to move smoothly into her world when I had ordered mine. Then Lawrence would never have existed.

We wandered through to the living-room and Anna collapsed into a comfortably misshapen armchair; a cool wind blew in through the french windows.

'Glorious! Glorious!' She flung back her head against a cushion. I didn't sit down.

'Why have you put up that awful photograph of me with the boys?' I stood, casually, swivelling it round the scarlet-headed drawing-pin.

'Don't you like it? It seemed so gay. I thought it could start my new board in Australia.' She giggled like a schoolgirl. 'Gerry says I only encouraged him to take this job because I don't have the moral strength to clear my board without a change of continents.'

I wanted Anna to be the reality of my life. The remembrance of my happy childhood and the hope for the future. Good hopeful love. Lawrence was the dark underside which would soon disappear. But not quite yet. I started to get restless and think of my little room. My little room and the telephone downstairs which I could hear, however loud I played the wireless. And which took me four rings to reach. Bounding down the stairs. Waiting, breath stopped, for His voice.

'I ought to be going.'

'It's Sunday, April. Stay to tea. You could help Gerry dig up the potatoes. He's decided we're all getting too fat so he's getting rid of them. That's why we had so many at lunch.'

'But you're going to Australia.'

'It's only for two years.'

How extraordinary, I thought, to be looking ahead for two whole years. 'I must go, I'm afraid.' I wanted to leave now with as much eagerness as before I had wanted to come.

'See yourself out, won't you. I'm just glued into this chair.'

'Right.' I turned back once. She lay as relaxed as a child with bare toes drooping like fingers.

'Don't forget the farewell scene in the departure lounge!' she called after me.

'I won't!' I slammed shut the front door which they never bothered to lock. I was not ready for Anna yet. Now I had seen her again, now I had assured myself she was the same, now I knew she would continue to be the same even if she was the other side of the world. Now I had no more need of her.

I started walking quickly. I would catch an empty Sunday train into London and sit in the corner seat, mysteriously aloof.

I froze myself into my London image and the warm colour of the dahlias disappeared into the back of my eyes.

7

SICILY

The beach lay behind fir trees, behind rows of pink and blue cabins. A little man, long sunburnt arms dangling out of a white singlet, came running. He talked excitedly and Lawrence talked too and waved a ticket.

Finally, together they put me into a cabin. I put my head out again quickly. In my enthusiasm for the moment I had forgotten Lawrence was leaving me. But his Italian seemed to have talked him right off the beach. I put on my bikini—chosen in girlish pink frills for him —and allowed myself to be placed under a flowering umbrella. Although the beach was small there were few people and no one very near me. The hot sun came through the parasol, impregnated the air all around me, pressed me into the sand. And the sand itself was hot. My body disappeared into tiny grains.

'You'll burn, I'm afraid.' The voice was high above me and sounded very concerned. I turned half over on my elbow and looked awkwardly skywards. The sun was blinding and I only saw black.

'The parasol was shading me,' I said defensively. Instead of the golden wood stem of my umbrella there was a long golden body.

'You must have gone to sleep. Can I join you?'

I sat up as it sat down.

'Of course.' It was Emmie. She curled up her legs beside

34

me so that only her projecting heels were visible. I made an effort to force myself into life.

'You're really quite red,' she started sorrowfully just as I was about to speak. 'It's strange you should have such very white skin when your hair is so black.'

'It's the Welsh blood in me,' I said once more defensively.

'Is Elizabeth Taylor Welsh? You look rather like her, you know. Or is that her husband?'

'Her husband,' I said stupidly. But now that I was upright and once more under shade, I was beginning to focus. The beach had become more brilliant; there were more umbrellas, more families with louder voices; the sand was yellower, the sky a deeper blue, the sea a deeper green; nearby a boy shouted '*Gelati! Gelati Motta!*' Now I recognized the scene. It was one of my abandoned postcards—with myself and Emmie crudely pasted on top. Or perhaps only myself, for Emmie, with her olive oil-coloured skin and nicotine hair disappeared into the sand.

'He's pure one hundred per cent male animal, Lawrence, don't you think?' She laughed and hugged her knees. 'Of course you know that. That's his attraction, isn't it?'

'I . . .' She looked at me sharply but I was nowhere near saying anything.

'Naturally that means he has all the male animal's faults as well.' Her drooping eyelids from which dark lashes sprang out theatrically hid her eyes as she stared vacantly at a young boy spreadeagled on the sand nearby. I wanted to stop her talking but I knew it was out of my control. I suspected her eyes were yellow. She was playing with me.

35

She rolled over suddenly onto her tummy: 'None of his friends believed his marriage would last for a moment. But it has, of course, for fifteen years. You don't think of breaking it up, do you?' Her voice was sharp as a needle. I could imagine her flicking tongue.

'I . . .' I kept my eyes fiercely shut.

'And then we realized that it's much better for him that way. He likes clean socks and things like that, you know. I remember one time we were together in Tunis and his case didn't arrive.' She edged her teeth along her fingers; I could hear the nostalgic clicking. 'In the end he wore my jeans. Of course he was slimmer then and I was fatter. He likes fat women, you know. Oh, please don't be offended. You've got a beautiful figure! I would never dream of saying Rubens or even Renoir . . . Yes, I got quite slim when I left him. Not that one ever really leaves someone like him. Just look at me now. I suppose in a way he's my oldest friend. Though don't misunderstand friend. Any real friendship has to have that element of sex, don't you agree? Besides, as I said before, he really is all male and it's a male prerogative to take the woman when he's in the mood. Don't you agree? Of course, it's lucky Enrico is the way he is, or perhaps if he wasn't, I wouldn't feel the need I do. *Dio mio!* It does sound complicated when it's truly so simple. You know I think we ought to buy you some calamine lotion. Of course one wouldn't admire a man if he didn't have a capacity for more than one woman, aren't I right? And if he can satisfy more, then he should have more. Now take last night, for a simple example of how useful an understudy can be. That's how I see myself, you know, just an understudy. You were tired, sleeping very heavily I believe, and I was awake. Of course . . .'

36

It was that final 'of course' that gave me the will to escape: 'Nothing in the world is "of course",' I said scrabbling hopelessly to my feet. 'I'm going for a swim.'

'Good idea,' I heard her say sympathetically as I teetered through the boiling sand. 'Salt water's the best thing for burning skin.'

I had forgotten the water wouldn't be an icy lash like an English sea, forcing out breath, out thought. These gentle greenish ripples were warm and slow. I walked out till the water reached my neck and then let my legs float up behind me. My flushed face disappeared beneath me and my hair rose to the surface in long undulating ropes. I had buried myself in the sun when Emmie was speaking and now I tried to bury the memory in the water. Already I had lost the words and intonation; only the sense still clung round me; Lawrence as usual but thicker and darker. I jerked my head up for air and kicked my legs in a wide-open scissor. There was no sense of surprise in me; no emotion ... I floated; water gave me a sense of isolation. Like a camel I would like to have buried my head in the sand; instead I stared at it with open eyes until I could see every golden ripple; they were like the hard furrows in a face.

8

ENGLAND

A room entirely of my own. Small, dark, a small dark hole which I burrow down and then dream.

I approach the flat with my eye fixed on my room. I pant as I approach and look over my shoulder like a rabbit who flees his captors; sensitive to the sound, the heavy tread. A man walks past my door, green door made secret with ivy curtain. He seems to look. I stop and wait, holding the keys silent in my pocket. My flat is best on a Sunday when the empty pavements reflect the empty sky, smooth and grey. The man passes and I open the door.

Up. Up. Up. The stairs wind me into myself till I unfurl chrysalis-like at the top. My spirits rise and float into music. Through the window—just a few roofs. An aerial or two, another person's window and the Sunday sky.

I choose a book. Oh, the ecstasy of independence!

I always enjoyed the long London bus journey from the station to my flat. And then the short walk of anticipation. The anticipation and immediate arrival was always best before Lawrence came down on me again.

I could sense his presence closing round me like a weather forecast. Sometimes he was an early morning haze, clinging, bewildered but not without its romantic appeal; at other times he was a white sea mist that rolled on top of me suddenly and carried with it a damp and dreary confusion; and at other times—the worst times which had been coming with alarming frequency lately —he was a heavy pea soup smog which plugged the pores in my body so that my skin tried to breathe and couldn't, tried to sweat and couldn't, and bound up my limbs so that they were like a mummy's swaddled tight against my sides; and like a mummy I had no eyes to see.

I was in my flat for a few moments of free tranquillity before it began to close round me. I used to be free from him for the longest period in my room but that was before we had made love there. Soon the sky would be blotted out; it would become dark and the self-pitying tears would pour from my inward-turned eyes.

I wished Jenny would come in. My bedroom was next door to hers; both above a little drawing-room, kitchen, bathroom below.

'Hi! Hi! Anybody there? April?' I could hear her stamping round downstairs. Piling up books. Pummelling cushions. She was tidy in an excess of energy. I tried to unmuffle my limbs or at least my voice.

'I'm upstairs.'

'Is that you? Good!' She started up the stairs. I loosened my arm enough to reach for a book.

'Reading. Reading. You would think you were the one who worked in a reputed firm of publishers!'

I acknowledged silently her employee's mockery of Lawrence's term. She had no idea of the relationship which she'd inaugurated. She was convinced that I was a dedicated intellectual with high principles. She reasoned there were no other motives for being a teacher. I put aside the Penguin Swinburne which I had grasped in des- peration—I had bought it for the pretty roses on the cover —and found the fog had lifted somewhat.

'Nice weekend?'

'Glorious! We planned the wedding date. March the thirty-first next year.'

'Avoiding April Fool's Day, I see.'

She sat down on my one chair and crossed her legs neatly. She wore a trouser suit tailored for town and her hair was wind-blown in the classical manner. She had fair hair and large blue eyes.

'Tom's decided to buy a new sailing boat ...'

The fog came down again and I stared at her blankly. This time only a telephone call could make it lift. For what else did I rush back to London? At six o'clock I reached for a bottle of sherry.

'Drink, Jenny?'

'No, thanks.' She simply didn't like the taste.

'Tom thinks he can get three weeks for our honeymoon.' She got up briskly as if the thought of marriage stimulated practical considerations: 'Have you seen the soap powder anywhere?'

I poured myself half a tumbler of sherry and felt better. The telephone rang. I jumped up.

'That'll be Tom!' I prepared myself. I picked up the phone. 'Yes, Tom. Hang on. I'll get her.'

I sat on the sofa listening to their conversation.

'No. I know it seems days ... I loved it ... every minute ... I simply must stay in ... but my clothes ... my washing ...'

I hunched up over my sherry willing Jenny to stay. Knowing she would go.

'All right then. But I must be back early.'

'I thought you were staying in,' I said grumpily.

'I should, but Tom says ...'

I poured myself some more sherry.

Nine o'clock was the worst time on a Sunday evening when Lawrence still hadn't rung and I had to leave the house before he even woke up.

Soon I started to cry.

The telephone rang.

'Hello,' I sobbed.

'Darling! I've been calling you all weekend. After you ran away like that. I was worried. I didn't know where you'd gone.' The tears dried on my cheeks leaving them stiff and crackly. I hadn't yet decided whether to let him know I was crying.

'I went home,' I said in neutral tones.

'Oh, darling! Are you angry with me? I felt so terrible about Julia coming back. I hate it anyway; but if you run away... Are you angry with me?'

Perhaps I had been angry. Perhaps tears of anger were drying on my face. It was a much more attractive quality than self-pity. I swallowed his bait. It was *me* who had made *him* unhappy. With his terrible wife.

'Oh, I'm not angry.'

'My darling! When can we meet? Tomorrow? I wish I could see you now. Hold you now. Kiss your white breasts.'

I swallowed.

'Tomorrow would be lovely. I don't have a lunch duty.'

'You are funny with your lunch duties. My beautiful creature with a lunch duty.' He played with a laugh, and I was laughing with him. Then his voice dropped into a low dreamy tone: 'Does school mean a lot to you? Have you a teaching vocation, my pure little nun? Sometimes you're solemn like a nun.'

I stood with the phone gripped fiercely in my hands and listened to his voice. How I loved him!

41

'Is that it? When you slip away to somewhere dark and deep, are you thinking about your forty children instead of me?'

9

SICILY

I surfaced again with my mouth gulping for air and there
was a face in front of me. It was a boy's face with round
coarse features and crooked white teeth. His black hair
dripped onto his shoulders. He started to talk to me but I
didn't understand him and I didn't want to talk to him
and I didn't like his leering face. It was too close to mine.
Now I saw there were other boys behind him—watching
and smiling. I blinked the water from my eyes. They were
children, only children.

'Go away!' I said loudly, turning my back on them and
trying to swim away. But another boy blocked my path
and I was tired. 'Don't be so stupid,' I said angrily as they
kept chattering and circling round me. 'I want to be
alone. Alone!' But instead of going, they came closer till
my legs touched one of them and then another and their
arms were brushing mine. My skin started to prickle.
'*Sola.* You understand? *Sola.*' But I couldn't shout and
paddle around at the same time; besides my voice only
made them smile more and their eyes gleam. It was ridiculous. I was hardly any distance from the shore. I would
turn myself firmly round and swim imperturbably shore-
wards. I swung round suddenly, kicking hard, ignoring
the contact with flesh, determined to get away. But instead I ran blindly head on into the original boy. His
expression was different now, the smile became all sneer

and with a long arm he lunged out towards me. 'No!' I shrieked, slapping out with my hand, for like a horrid monstrous animal he was pulling, jerking, prodding at my bikini pants. 'No!' I shrieked, but my flailing arm only sent up a great splash of water and made the boys, swimming eagerly round, laugh uproariously. I twisted myself; flung myself backwards until my nose and mouth were full of water. But he had a grip on the edge of my pants and his fingers were like feelers. They slipped down my open legs and I couldn't close them, or I would have sunk. A hard finger poked at my softest part. 'No! No!' I was gasping and shuddering, sick with the sea water, sick with his touch. Perhaps if I was sick they would leave me. But then I would drown. Where were the pretty coloured beach huts? Where was help? Where was Emmie?

I must have shouted. Perhaps I had seen her coming. And the boys disappeared as cleanly as driftwood before a ship. She took my arm and drew me in. I was only a yard or two out of my depth.

'You'll have to learn about things,' she said, still holding my arm as I coughed and spluttered. 'Sicilian boys are so admiring of foreign girls.'

I stopped choking and let her lead me to the beach. I collapsed onto my towel and she was watching me still. 'Of course, it's really a compliment to your powers of attraction.'

As I got my breath again I thought I couldn't bear her to patronize me; to know my panic—more than she did already:

'A ludicrous scene,' I said, trying to smile.

'Oh no. Not ludicrous.' She sat down beside me and using her own towel rubbed lightly at the ends of my hair. 'I thought you looked frightened. As if you thought they would rape you.' She opened her eyes wide and laughed.

I laughed too. But my eyes were small and red with the salt water.

'I was terrified of drowning,' I said. 'More than losing my virtue.'

'You are frightened of the sea?'

'Not usually.'

'I see.' With an expression of objective fact-seeking, 'The English then are not all sea-loving islanders?'

That sounded odd to me and I remembered she was English herself. So Lawrence had said. Where was he? I hadn't called out for him.

'I have an idea.' She was up again above my feet. 'I'll buy you a cognac. That would be good after your shock, don't you think? And they sell such nice miniature bottles here.' And then over her shoulder with a smile: 'If anyone approaches you, make a resolute sign of the cross.'

The moment she was out of sight behind the fir trees I went to my cabin and locked the door. I sat there in the cool dark box and heard my heart beating. Gradually it became softer and the noises from the beach louder. My eyes became accustomed to the gloom so I got out my powder compact and eyebrow pencil. I looked steadily at my face in the little mirror. So, some badly brought up children had been playing games with me in the water... So, Lawrence had been playing games with ... My face was pink and glowing. I thought it would become a rich brown. I smoothed my eyebrows into sweeping black wings. And the unaccustomed colour would turn me from an English moth to a brilliant brazen humming-bird. No one would guess at my roots. No one would think me a school teacher.

10

ENGLAND

I walk to school from my room in the morning. And I am submerged in the sense of other daily workers. A few trees over my head. A dog barks. The pavement moves under our feet like a conveyorbelt. And I am part of it. I am part of the rush of early workers. I gain power and momentum from them and lose my own midget purposes. I look forward to the bell ringing and the school forming into undulating lines. The prayer, O Lord. The re-assembly into class. I understand the order and sublimate myself.

I am a teacher. I am a nun. With my vocation set apart from the rest of the world.

I taught in a primary school in a dirty beautiful part of London—a square blue patch beside the oily waters of Paddington canal and beyond the shiny construction of new buildings set on the still ravaged remains of the old.

My pupils were Irish immigrants, poor English and a few negroes. Their fathers, labourers, were building up the area round us. When I set an essay entitled 'Home', Pat and Jo and others wrote about their bare feet in the bogs. And Lenny and Grace and others wrote about the burning sun. They were all born in London. I walked to work because the smell in a bus gave me a headache—especially if I had a hangover. If it was a Lawrence lunch day I carried with me pretty shoes and earrings. I was self-conscious of being from a classier background than the other teachers and imagined I wanted to be accepted as one of them. I pretended to be as interested in conversations about the best place to buy bacon as they seemed to be. But they were old or ugly or man-to-man.

Even when I had allayed their suspicions that I was a supply teacher; even when they saw my hands became as inky as theirs; my face as sweaty and my legs as thick, they never quite accepted me.

'Good morning, Miss Leventon!' The head was small and scurrying like the white rabbit. Permanently surprised at his successful struggle to headmastership, he was also wary of me. He probably guessed my father was on the school board. But I wanted him to accept me too.

'Good morning, Mr Chitty! May I take the children to the park today?'

He looked down ponderously at his habitual pile of primers.

'Let's check the weather first, shall we?' He smiled at this restrained use of power over a subordinate and passed fussily on. But I did want him to like me.

'Morning!' The teachers' room. Inspired to teach. I hung up my coat and poured out a cup of tea. What tea! Sweet, thick and black; so black it needed a stream of milk to turn it pale. My stomach rumbled in anticipation at the familiar smell.

'Morning, April!'

'Morning, all!' I had to admit it. I was the pick of the bunch, set apart in my secret beauty and youth. They weren't sure where I came from. They didn't know where I went at lunch time. They suspected I led a strange life to them; foreign and glamorous. Once Lawrence came to school—so tall, so distinguished. They thought he might have been my father. But they were never quite certain.

I blew on my tea. I tied my hair back into a rubber band. After all, mostly they thought I was a teacher.

'Morning, Iris!'

Iris was dressed in one of her two Terylene pleated skirts with toning short-sleeved sweater and sensible brown shoes to match her sensible brown hair. At first I had tried to imitate this dedicated teacher's style. But a too easy butterfly-to-moth success had sent me scurrying back to dolly-rockers. Except for the rubber band. I imagined it a symbol of my earnest purpose to teachers, head and children.

'Morning, Jill!'

Jill had more of a face than Iris and less of a body. She enjoyed teaching religious knowledge and arithmetic, while Iris adored geography and gym. Jill disguised her face in the same way Iris disguised her body; she combed her hair so that it fell beige and straight across her face like an elegant pair of curtains. She was always happy on Mondays, because her first class was Religious Knowledge.

'Morning, Mrs Smith!'

Mrs Smith was old and out of control. She only kept her place at the school because she had been there so long that the parents felt a comfortable sense of tradition when she appeared at end-of-term meetings. She taught the smallest children and her arms were full of bottle tops and matchboxes and her old fingernails coloured with plasticine and glue. She made the tea for us.

'Morning, John!'

In romantic moods I saw John as D. H. Lawrence. He was thin and dark and intense and might have grown a

48

beard any day. I imagined the passionately emotional life he lived under his teacher's surface of frowning eyes, busy hands and bent shoulders. He was dreadfully self-conscious when he talked to me so that I presumed myself an important part of his passionate hidden depths. John, young-old, elbow-patched tweed coat, escorted us ladies to the assembly room.

'Let's hope there's more of my class than there was last week,' I said, like many a teacher before me.

'The head tells me next year the average class will be down to thirty-eight,' John, as the only male teacher, had a special relationship with the head and parcelled out news to us women with considerate self-importance.

The assembly room was the newest part of the school and had bright glass windows. I stationed myself on a small strip of ground which was cast in shadow by a netball post on the playground outside. I had discovered it one atrocious hangover morning. The children sported a varied uniform of grubby grey. They wore the same thick wool socks summer and winter and when it was very cold or very hot their legs above them turned pink and mottled. The boys' faces were red and knocked from early morning fights and the girls, who sat holding each other's hands and gossiping, wore cat-like looks of self-satisfaction. I tried not to separate them into individuals until later in the day when I felt a bit stronger. On bad hangover mornings I would shut my eyes during the prayers and only half open them afterwards. On good mornings I sang the hymn loudly and looked stern.

We dispersed to our classrooms.

Forty-two—all present—nine-year-old children waited for me to restore order. It was easier by Wednesday, hard again by Friday.

'Reading. Book two, page thirty-three.'

'Miss, we've read this before.'

'Thank you, Grace. We will read it again. Pat first. Then Lenny. Then John. Then Paul.'

'What about the girls, miss?'

'Then Grace.'

'Bbb but ... the old man ... found it ... hard ... to el ... le ... vate.'

'All right, Pat. Next.'

'Elevate the bag which lay across his ...' A loud fluent voice which I should have begun with.

'Miss! It was me next. Not John.'

'You've missed your turn then. Hard luck.'

'John always reads. It's not fair, miss.'

The muttering swelled. Jamie dropped a ruler. Catherine was hit with a flying rubber and put up her hand self-righteously. Jim at the next desk grabbed her arm and tried to pull it down. She shrieked.

'Miss!'

A crescendo had been reached. I sighed.

'If you can't behave, none of you will read. I will.'

I took up the book and assumed an interested tone:

'But the old man found it hard to elevate the bag which ...'

'We've read that before, miss. Twice before, miss.'

But after a while they listened and I had a moment to think. On the whole a bad thing. It was the first time I had thought about Lawrence since I arrived at school. Immediately it became an obsession. My voice rose and moved more quickly. My knees gripped tensely together. I looked forward to our lunch meeting with despairing anticipation. My darling lover ...

'... but the dog was too small to see the old man ...'

50

'Miss! Miss! Please, miss!'

'The bell's gone. Miss! It's gym!'

They threw themselves out of their clothes revealing enormous thick bloomers.

'Miss! I've got a splinter in my foot. Can I stay up here?'

'I've got a bruise on my knee.'

'I've got a verruca.'

'Everyone downstairs, whether they're doing gym or not.'

Forty-two children and I was less aware of them than I was of Lawrence's shoe-lace.

'My mother said I shouldn't ...'

'Downstairs!' I sighed. I tried so hard to be a 'teacher'. Iris's class paraded the corridors in neat files. Mine ran. I yapped hopelessly at their heels: 'Walk! Walk! Lenny! Single file! Patricia! On the left!'

They burst into the assembly room and as usual the wide empty space seemed to go to their heads. Hoola hoops whizzed dangerously across the floor.

Although shaming, it was a relief when Mr Chitty felt obliged to restore order in person. He did it for me about once every three weeks—always on Mondays.

'Children!' He came in the door quietly, hardly raising his voice and yet there was instant silence. I stood meekly beside him. He came up with me to the classroom and waited till they were bent quietly over their next lesson.

'No park, I think, today, Miss Leventon.' He smiled sweetly at me without a hint of reproach and shut the door gently behind him. Soon afterwards it was break and then only two more classes before lunch.

It was not surprising after such a morning that Lawrence found me romantically pale and undemanding. It was sheer exhaustion. He sat in his car round the corner from the school. He had a manuscript with him. As usual he looked delighted to see me as if the separation had been an unbearable misery.

'Darling!' He leant across to open the door for me and then drew me, weak and unresisting into his arms. 'Darling, you look so *distraite*, a little less absolutely glowing than I expect. Have those horrible children been misusing ...'

'You know I love my children ...'

But he kissed me very gently, already weaving his own fantasy about my condition and needs. I could see him deciding we would have a lovingly gentle lunch—somewhere remote and pale.

I kissed him back, sweet and tired. His arm was heavy and protective. I tried not to cry in the first ten seconds of our meeting.

'Home was a strain,' I said.

'Wait. Don't tell me yet. I'll drive us somewhere first.'

'Let's have a picnic.'

'My darling romantic creature.'

We lay on the grass in Regent's Park and I was self-conscious as Lawrence looked at me with his bright eyes and licked his lips. It was warm and we had a bottle of wine. He pushed me behind a tree and started to kiss me.

'No! Lawrence.'

He put a hand on my thigh. I felt the eyes of the park turning on us. I had taken off my elastic band and he was pulling my hair round my face over his. Running it through his lips.

'No, Lawrence!' I thought of the other teachers, the school. It was getting late.

'Forbidden. Forbidden fruit. Aren't you, my darling?' He sat up and pushed back his hair. The wrinkles round his eyes spread out in the sun.

'How's publishing?' I asked to divert him from my own flushed face and shiny eyes. I had to get back to school.

'I hear your friend's engaged. We talked about you this morning.' He smiled conspiratorially.

'I've got to get back.' My head ached. He would go to his comfortable office with his manuscripts and his secretary. I had my forty-two children.

'Miss! Where've you been? Mrs Smith brought us in from the playground, miss.'

'You look red, miss.'

'Miss is blushing.'

'Miss! Can I go to the toilet, please, miss?'

'Tom doesn't really want to go to the toilet, miss. He's only just been. He wants to make an ink pellet, miss.'

I wrote on the blackboard in very large letters: 'Anyone who is still talking when I finish writing will do Exercise Ten in their arithmetic book.' I turned round to complete silence.

'History book. Page one hundred and eighty,' I said briskly. It was a trick no true teacher would have employed. I sighed for the end of the day.

'Can I collect the crayons?'

'Can I walk to the corner with you?'

'I love your stockings, miss.'

I collected my books. Tidied my desk. Looked round the classroom unable, as usual, to believe I had arrived only that morning—or that I could possibly arrive there again the next morning.

'Good day, John.' He was waiting for me in the corridor. I was tired. I smiled weakly.

'I wondered whether you might like to go to the cinema sometime?'

I was surprised. Tired but surprised. I tried to look at him objectively, prospectively, but I had seen his mannerisms for too long: honest hesitant eyes, indecisive mouth, dark shadowed cheeks where the beard might grow, and thin wavering hands. Without charm. I hadn't expected his hidden depths to rise to the surface.

'There's an Ingmar Bergman season on at the N.F.T.' Charmless with a rod of steel down his tweed back.

'Sometime,' I replied unenthusiastically.

II

SICILY

The door jerked protestingly against its hinges. The thin slatted wood shivered under heavy hands knocking worriedly.

'April! April! Are you all right in there?'

'Oh, hello!' I was gay and lively behind the closed door. 'Just on my way out. Did you meet Emmie with my sad story? And a brandy?' I opened the door laughing at the world.

Lawrence stood outside wearing navy blue towelling shorts. His large hairless chest swelled above them. It already seemed to be a confident brown, but I could tell by the hunched-up set of his shoulders that he had only just lost a hang-dog anxiety.

'It was so ridiculous,' I said determinedly as he kissed me like a warm-hearted father on the cheek. 'They were all round me like little minnows, terribly young. Still, I'm glad Emmie saved me from a fate worse than death. She was wonderful.'

'She shouldn't have let you swim alone.' Lawrence took my arm. 'And how pink you are, too.'

'It'll go brown very soon.' I threw my arms above my head, restoring myself to the position of gay young thing, beautiful (though just now a little over-done), untroubled, no trouble: 'I want this to go on for ever!'

Laughing with relief, Lawrence pinched the back of my neck.

'Careful! You'll have all the lusting Sicilians after you again.' And as he half shook me I saw behind us on the sand, oiled and gleaming Emmie, sun worshipping, eyes closed.

'Lunch-time!' announced Lawrence.

'Lunch-time!' I echoed dutifully.

'Oh!' said Emmie, opening her eyes. 'April. Did Lawrence bring you your brandy? He said he would.'

'He revived me himself.'

'Is that so?'

'Enrico is meeting us,' said Lawrence. 'At the Charleston. With a friend.'

'Not at the Charleston. *And* with a friend!' Emmie grimaced.

The Charleston looked like a Mississippi river-boat built on a pier between the various lidos. The hallway was decorated with enthusiastic potted palm trees. Enrico stepped out smoothly from behind one of the most enthusiastic. His friend took longer to disentangle himself from the fronds. He was very small and slight with brilliant green eyes in a dark brown face. His lips by contrast were particularly pale and delicate like a child's. Enrico waved a cigar.

'Well, well! Tatti, here does not, I'm afraid, speak any English.'

'He doesn't look as if speaking is his strong point in any language,' said Emmie brightly.

Just before we reached the dining-room, Lawrence held me back apologetically, 'Not much fun for you, I'm afraid.'

What did he imagine my lunches were away from him? A froth of juvenile curls—oh, youth!—heads bent like mechanical pecking birds over pot and pills, rocking with

laughter, wild out-of-this-world ideas. He had once pub-
lished a book called *Whizz for Kids*, I remembered. 'Never
mind,' he said comfortingly, while Emmie informed the
waiter that she wouldn't eat anything if they didn't have
fresh *griglia*—for wasn't that the point of Sicily? And
while Enrico talked languorous Italian to Tatti, 'Never
mind. We'll be off alone tomorrow.'

'Off where?' I asked.

But he was too involved with the wine list for an
answer.

12

ENGLAND

I am a creature who moves at night, flies over the city with gossamer wings outspread. My eyes are painted like glowing bulbs of deepest green that see where others see only black. In the red of the sunset I am burnt and I am born.

They try and catch me, hold me down to earth. Grasp in their heavy fists my silken folds and flying satin. But my eyes dazzle them, mingle with the stars and the city blocks of light till at length the lids begin to droop, droop and shade the light. They pounce then. Grapple. Think that now's their chance.

I slip away. Pale creature, black hair flowing. I leave them—poor dull objects, alone and crying for what they cannot have.

Preparations for an evening on the town lasted me at least an hour and a half. Since school finished earlier than most jobs I had the time.

I filled my room with abandoned clothes and the bathroom with essence of pine. I liked the water to be a deep dark green and so hot that drops of water trickled off the mirror.

Then I flung open the little window in my room and lay flaccid on my bed. All the time I watched jealously for the first signs of night. The deepening of the sky sent my spirits soaring. As it darkened I'd bring out my bottles and creams and hair tonics and clippers and pluckers; lay them out ready for creation.

I liked late summer better than early summer because it was dark sooner. And cloudy evenings better than bright ones.

I sat at my table with my little silver mirror nostalgic-ally warped with age and gave myself a new personality. I believed in this creature I was creating. The green, silver-shadowed lids, the black spikes of sable lashes, the cheek-bones made prominent with white above and rose below, the mouth silky smooth with oil and the teeth white brushed again and again. I did the face first to give it time to feel its new shape.

And then the body. It was an art even to choose which clothing it deserved. I pulled out a short red satin slip and then a white pyjama suit and finally with satisfaction a pair of striped trousers and a white lace blouse. My hair, I decided, would be smooth like a tailor's dummy. Tied back with a piece of floating silk.

I met Jenny downstairs. I spared her a moment. She looked up from the *Evening Standard*.

'Smashing! New blouse?'

'God, no. I've had it for years.'

'Good day?' Jenny affected a pair of horn-rimmed glasses for reading. Now she looked at me through them and her eyes seemed narrowed by the heavy frames.

'My boss was talking about you today. I didn't think he knew you that well.'

'What well?' I shifted a hip easily. I was confident in my face and body which glistened in such obvious self-sufficiency. 'I must fly.'

'Anywhere nice?'

59

'Festival Hall. Dinner.'

I caught a taxi on the corner of the street. All the spare money I had went on taxis. In the evenings it helped to preserve my image.

I loved to sit back with the night city rushing by me. I even liked arriving with the other taxis and other evening people.

Then I had to wait till I was in my seat and the lights dimmed and the orchestra began. I had read somewhere that girls didn't feel alone at concerts. But I did until the lights had dimmed.

The music filled my head with new dreams. I didn't watch the conductor. I shut my eyes and saw my own passionate nature reflecting in the music. When the lights came up for the interval, I blinked theatrically and when I stood up held the arm of the seat as if shaken.

In the bar I stood apart and special, staring negligently at others before they stared at me. The last piece had been a Mozart serenade for wind instruments. I ran my finger round the rim of my glass and tried to make a pure note.

'April!'

I relied absolutely on my cloak of anonymity. This coarse pronouncing of my name had a shattering effect. I stood in its harsh spotlight. The rich make-up I had applied with such conviction became a heavy plaster cast which threatened to choke me. I wanted to claw it from my face. My magic clothes became a ludicrous fancy dress.

'Hello, John!'

'If I had known you were coming tonight. You are by yourself, aren't you? I thought so but I waited a bit before I was sure. I was watching you.'

He had been watching me as I stood in my cloak of anonymity, luxuriating in my freedom and independence.

He had been watching me—this little man still in his tweed patched coat he wore as a teacher; unwashed, unchanged, waiting to drag me into his own squalid little world.

'It's been a terrific first half, don't you think?'

'Time to go back, I think.' I put my drink conclusively on the bar. I pulled my hair around my face. I shook my trouser leg, pointed a pretty foot. 'The man I was coming with fell ill.' How I despised myself!

'Perhaps we can meet afterwards, then?' He jumped beside me as I glided up the shallow steps. Hurrying faces noted the disparity in our images.

'We meet tomorrow anyway,' I said for their benefit and laughed—for their benefit.

'I've eaten dinner, but perhaps we could share a cup of tea or a sandwich. I've always room for a sandwich.' He laughed cosily.

No escape. No escape.

'We'll meet after then.' Gaily I agreed and took my seat. My changed seat—a lonely teacher's seat with memories of the grubby day behind and the dreary day in front and the sandwich and the cup of tea already brewing in some Corner House.

I cried as the music filled the faces round me with contentment. Then I took off my long floating silk scarf and the gold belt clasped round my hips. I knew John wouldn't notice the difference. He looked at my face, at the expression of the docile lamb being led to the slaughter. He smiled with victory.

'We can walk over the bridge if you like, or the underground's easy from here.'

We walked back over the bridge which I had flown across before and found on the other side a nice coffee bar.

'I think they do espresso,' he said as we sat down. 'Have you noticed how difficult it's suddenly become to get espressos in London?'

The lights were low and when our coffees came and they were espressos he became more relaxed.

'You find it rather hard sometimes with the children, don't you? I mean, of course, it is difficult with a big class—particularly when they're more boys than girls like in yours. I wonder if you'd mind if I gave you a bit of advice?'

'No. Of course not.'

'I didn't want to offend you. The thing is it's no good being severe after they're misbehaving. You've got to be severe from the moment you walk through the door. Then if they're very good, you can let up a bit, but never, never the other way round.'

I tried to smile.

'It sounds easy.'

He drank a draught of coffee self-deprecatingly.

'The trouble is you've got too nice a nature.' Then he found his teacher's role had drawn him into a dangerous intimacy and he took another sudden gulp of coffee and choked on it.

I looked sympathetic. Soon I would go. I had decided on a plan.

'No, really. I'm very happy on my own.' I made him leave me at the bus stop, though it quite upset his sense of procedure. 'Thanks for the coffee,' I shouted after him in a sudden feeling of unnecessary apology. After all, he was content. And then I hailed a taxi. It was the only way to restore my image.

Lawrence's house was in Hampstead and it had a garden with a wall round it and an iron grille gate. Through the grille the house was clearly visible and since it was protected from the road by the garden, the curtains were often left undrawn even late at night.

I stood by the grille and carefully opening my handbag took out my scarf and gold belt and restored them to their rightful position. But the house was dark. I walked up and down in front of the wall and my trousers twined round my legs and my scarf trailed along behind me. A clock struck midnight. I thought, romantically, it came from the church where Keats was buried. But still I saw nothing in the house. It was late; perhaps they were in bed. Lawrence would be wearing the striped pyjamas he affected to dislike so much because she had chosen them—and probably his glasses too if he was having a last minute read. He never let me see him in them. Or they might be talking about their friend's dinner party. Lawrence complaining about the effect of jugged hare on his delicate constitution or how all their friends seemed suddenly so old and dowdy. How lucky I was to be outside the house. It hit me with a shock of happiness. I passed the iron grille for the last time and started briskly along the pavement.

A taxi drew up behind me.

'Got a two shilling bit, darling?'

My feet carried me mechanically on. My heart grew legs and pounded along ahead.

'Here you are. Do you know it's half past twelve? I'd no idea it was so late.'

I heard the grille gate swing shut behind them. And Lawrence's voice saying gaily:

'If one more person congratulates me on running an independent publishers ...'

'You'll what?' She sounded amused. 'Have you got a key?'

'I'll advertise for bids in *The Sun*.'

'You are a hypocrite, Larry. An inebriated one, too.'

The front door slammed on their good spirits. And then in order to drain my cup to the full I hired the taxi they'd just left. It still smelt of Lawrence and some sophisticated female scent. On the whole, I thought, I'd had my money's worth that evening.

13

SICILY

'A divine interlude!' exclaimed Emmie after lunch, who had only nipped at a geranium ornamenting the table and sipped at a Punt è Mes. Her big eyes lolled round the table, passing her husband and his friend with a slight contraction—their chairs were closer than before—until they rested on me. I glanced at Lawrence who lay back in his chair fanning himself with the wine list. Emmie's eyes followed mine.

'Ah!' she said quite softly. 'It looks like we two have the only bodies with energy, the only free spirits.'

As a matter of fact I did not feel particularly energetic. My skin was hot with sunburn and my eyelids felt swollen. For once I could have happily joined Lawrence in his siesta. Nevertheless, when Emmie uncurled gracefully to her feet (I saw with new surprise how tall she was), when she held out her long fingers towards me, I got up at once.

'I'm taking April from you, Larry.' She tapped him playfully on the forehead. 'But do not fear, she will return as pure a lamb as she is now.'

I didn't want to go with her. I wanted an excuse to take the place of strength of mind. I looked at Lawrence beseechingly, but he only laughed and pouted his mouth in a kiss to me:

'I shall be raging for you like a tiger when you return.'

'I will show her my Palermo,' said Emmie.

Immediately outside the restaurant she summoned a taxi. Her mood seemed to have changed entirely. Perhaps she felt able to relax, now her captive was secure. She sank into the seat and ran her hand up the back of her hair.

'It is really too hot,' she complained petulantly. 'Perhaps first we will get cool. I can see you too do not enjoy walking hot streets.'

The taxi drove back into the centre of Palermo. Emmie seemed too tired to talk and once she had given directions to the driver closed her eyes. Only her draped limbs swung with the movement of the car.

14

ENGLAND

On Friday I left school after the mid-morning break. Lawrence would come to pick me up for lunch and find the bird had flown. What might he not imagine! It was a fitting rebuke for his daring to enjoy a party in the company of his wife.

Anna was leaving for Australia that day and there was to be a family farewell.

'We thought you weren't coming!'

My parents kept a small flat in London. It was now filled with my mother in a black ribbed coat, as if in mourning, who immediately placed a large cardboard box in my hands; Anna, as nearly harassed as she could ever be, and Christopher and Timothy in their usual obstreperous mood. I put down the package and helped Anna stuff their flailing arms into their coats.

'Thanks, April. Oh, God! Have you seen my hat anywhere? We're being met by a representative of the firm and Gerry said I must look decent.'

'I gave it to April,' exclaimed my mother excitedly.

The hat was found in the cardboard box I had pushed under the table.

'Isn't that your going-away hat?'

'What?' She looked up from writing out labels and taking the hat from my hands jammed it onto her head. 'Yes, I suppose it is.'

The scarlet hat reminded me of her wedding day. The night she left I had cried so hard into my bed that I had to change the pillow-case and the top sheet.

'Where's father?' I asked as we collected up the cases and the porter pressed on Anna a little something his wife had made specially.

'He's meeting us at the airport,' said my mother anxiously.

Father surprised me in his dark city suit and well-brushed bowler. He stood at the B.O.A.C. desk with a large bunch of flowers.

'I thought you deserved something beautiful from England.' He handed them to Anna. They were long white lilies. It was the sort of gesture which surprised people who didn't know him and had won him my mother.

'I'm hungry,' shouted Christopher.

'So am I!' yelled Timothy.

'You'll get plenty to eat on the plane,' said my mother. But for the sake of peace we bought them a large ice cream each. Which left the burden of conversation on us. The adults. We had nothing to say.

'Don't use those horrible airmail letters when you write,' I began eventually.

'They're so much cheaper,' said my mother.

My father brushed the top of his hat.

'Excuse me,' said a small Indian passing by, 'is there exit?' We all three pointed in different directions and he set off eagerly.

'Look at the ice cream on Timothy's face,' said Anna. 'Just hold the flowers for a moment would you, April?'

'That's your flight number being called,' said my father.

'Oh, darling!' Mother's eyes were bright. Her voice choked. Anna hugged her comfortingly as if she were the mother. She received father's bear hug and kissed me cheek to cheek.

'Come over, all of you! All of you ...'

'We're going! We're going to Australia!' shrieked the children delightedly while mother cried and father looked serious and I stood at the barrier watching them go with the flowers which we had all forgotten clasped to my breast. And then they had walked through customs control and gone.

'Gone!' said my father bracingly. He took mother's arm and then mine, so he stood between us like a sailor with two girls. 'How about cheering ourselves up over a late luncheon?'

It was a strange experience sitting with my parents in the *Tavern in the Sky*. Father ordered a bottle of wine after a good deal of consultation with the waiter. His bowler sat on the spare seat beside him.

'I'm sorry about the flowers, father,' I said. They lay by the bowler hat. The petals were already starting to turn yellow at the edges.

'What, dear?'

Mother had gone to the ladies and when she came back her cheeks were painted a brave pink.

'The plane should be taking off,' said father closely studying his watch.

'Yes.' Mother looked down and then turned to me brightly, 'Was it hard getting away from school, dear?'

'I arranged it ages ago. Then Mr Chitty doesn't panic.'

'Do headmasters panic?' said father doubtingly.

'He's only just a headmaster.'

'Only just, dear. I thought he had been there for years.'

'I meant qualitatively just, mother.'

Their attempt at communicating with me petered into

a dismal silence. I was hardly in the mood to encourage it. I knew it was only a diversion for them.

'Quite a reasonable wine,' said father, emptying the bottle into his glass with *pater familias* high-handedness which reminded me of Lawrence. 'I gather employers bring their guilty secrets here.' An ironic echo of my own thoughts. Lawrence had once suggested lunch at London Airport.

'Just coffee for me,' I said from behind the menu, suddenly feeling unable to cope with my parents and my thoughts at the same closely confined table.

'Well, I hope April doesn't marry someone with ambitions abroad,' said my mother suddenly.

'I don't expect I'll marry at all,' I mumbled.

'Come now!' said my father heartily.

'I might be dedicated to teaching,' I said experimentally in my father's office car that took us back into London.

'Oh, no!' My mother fondled my hand in vague protest.

'No hope of that,' said my father cheerfully.

'Goodbye!' I kissed my parents carefully which was all I could offer in comfort or farewell. I got out of the car remembering not to slam the door which my father hates. 'Thanks for the lift.'

Well, at least they had each other. I climbed the stairs to the flat, and when I reached the top the doorbell rang. So I turned round again.

'Oh, hello!'

Lawrence looked as unhappy as I could have hoped.

'I waited outside your school. I thought you must be ill till I saw you come in.' He didn't feel he had a right to reproach me or lessen my freedom. But I never used the power it gave me over him.

'I couldn't let you know. I'm sorry. I was seeing my

sister off at the airport.'

At once his old eyes regained their lustre; the droop to his mouth became world-weary rather than dog-like and dejected. He was wearing a particularly beautiful brown linen suit with a dark blue shirt. Clothes maketh man; I sighed at the sight of him.

'I had planned a special lunch,' he said gaily, seeing me looking at his suit. 'But since you put family ties first I was forced to enjoy it by myself.'

'Come in,' I said. My heart, my exhibitionist heart, immediately pounding at his smile and his closeness. The lethargy of sadness disappearing in a moment.

'Don't you want to know where I went?' he said, following up the stairs behind me and then touching my hip with his hands.

'No!' I said breathlessly. 'No. I don't.' I wasn't really answering because I knew we would make love in my room before Jenny came home and I couldn't think of anything else. We reached my room.

'Well!' he said. 'I shall tell you anyway.' He crossed beside the bed and drew the curtains. 'When we are in bed together and you can't escape all the thrilling details of what you missed.'

'Undress me!' I said, throwing myself shamelessly on the bed.

'How civil of you to invite me,' returned Lawrence, disposing eagerly of his own clothes. The emptiness of the morning was filled.

We lay side by side. He had been for lunch to the Playboy Club in Park Lane. I asked him whether it was very good for his publisher's image and he said that it would take a publisher to recognize a publisher and then it would be a question of who drew first. Which reminded me:

71

'Shouldn't you be in the office?' But that wasn't my business.

'I'm the boss.' It was Jenny's description.

'My sister is so beautiful,' I whispered involuntarily. 'I'm glad you've never met her.'

'Dog in the manger.'

We went to sleep.

Jenny woke us up. She came in downstairs with end-of-day dumpings, and Lawrence scrambled into his clothes so nervously that for a moment I was able to laugh at him. But then I stopped because it seemed like mocking myself too, and besides Jenny might come up to look for me. I would have to divert her attention while he slipped down the stairs.

'My darling!' Lawrence said a little distractedly, but I admired him for the effort.

'I can't see you tomorrow, but I'll telephone.'

So I kissed him gently in our endless stream of farewells and went down to Jenny.

'Hi!' she said. 'Anna go off all right?'

'Yes. She went all right.'

'Tom's got a friend with him tonight.' Jenny smiled cheeringly and I heard Lawrence pass the door. 'Want to come with us?'

'What's he like?' I began and then added with loud enthusiasm mostly to drown Lawrence's banging exit: 'Yes, I'd love that! I feel like dancing. We couldn't persuade them into a night-club, could we?'

'Oh, yes! Perhaps if we both try ... They're coming at eight; we can eat first and then go on. There's a place ...'

Jenny loved making plans; so did her future husband. I imagined their marriage as one enormous schedule— with commercial breaks when one or the other of them had an affair. They were very socially-sexually orientated. Perhaps after all their affairs would be all part of the schedule—wife-swapping with their best friends. That's of course where Tom's friend came in. I wondered what he was like. Jenny was still planning:

'... but only of course if you like him.'

I wondered without much interest what she had been suggesting because Jenny was in truth clean-living and pure-hearted. An incision through her healthy chest would have revealed a neat pink heart with MARRIAGE embroidered across it.

'I'll look out the glad rags, then.'

15

SICILY

The car stopped quite suddenly outside a large stone palazzo built above the narrow and crowded street. A line of Fiats immediately formed behind us, each driver roaring up to the queue, screeching to a halt and finally slamming a fist on his horn.

'God!' Emmie flung up a long golden arm to her head and then thrust a note to the taximan.

'I'm sorry you're not feeling well.'

'Ghastly!' She led me through a courtyard behind the stone façade and up a flight of stone stairs. Someone opened a door to us, but it was so dark that at first I could hardly tell in what sort of place we had arrived. Gradually, as my eyes opened again after the glare outside, I saw that we were in a very large high-ceilinged room. Emmie was talking to a young girl in a white apron—it was she who had let us in—they spoke in Italian so I couldn't understand.

'Well, how do you like my lair?' She kicked her sandals into the air. The maid disappeared backwards into the shadows.

'I thought your house was burnt down?'

'Like a delicious cool tomb, isn't it? I never open the shutters.' She shivered exaggeratedly. 'I expect the furniture is turning white like plants kept without sun.'

But there was no furniture. Now I could see the red walls hung with woven material and the flagged floor patterned with rugs and cushions—otherwise nothing.

The sudden contrast from heat to cool, from light to dark, had disorientated me. I found I was swaying slightly as I stood there. I couldn't remember exactly how much wine I had drunk at lunch but it was certainly more than I was used to. My head felt extremely heavy, yet at the same time my body was wide awake. Without being able to properly see Emmie, I was intensely aware of her.

'Well,' she said, 'aren't you glad we left those brutes?'

'It's so quiet here ...' I could feel my legs tingling slightly from the change of temperature. My dress, become cooler and drier, no longer clung to my back.

'Come, we will have our siesta together.'

I could see Emmie now as she crouched down on her heels among the thick pile of a fur carpet and crowed at me through her long curving neck: 'Watch how I teach you to be a true Sicilian.'

Side by side we lay down on the rug which, though so thick, seemed to carry to our bodies the coldness of the stone flagging. I felt a lack of grace in me beside Emmie's easily coiled limbs.

'Let me help you,' she said. 'Take off your dress; such a pretty dress so sweet and fresh-looking, so young ...' Her voice lowered and softened, '... so plump and soft.' She crooned to me as she took off my dress. 'Look,' she said wonderingly, I could imagine her eyes wide in the dark, 'look, little yellow grains of sand brought in the warm crease under your arm all the way from the sea shore. What a lovely place to be; what a lucky piece of sand!'

16

ENGLAND

Our flat had become a battleground of smells. My favoured pine bath essence fought bravely with Jenny's sweet-scented apricot soap. Sugary hair spray deferred to the acrid smell of nail varnish and in the drawing-room six joss sticks overwhelmingly and perhaps fortunately defeated our own personal eau de toilette. We had prepared ourselves for an evening on the town with the dedication and subtlety of fading whores. Even Jenny, who usually tended to classical simplicity, for once had allowed herself to be carried away. At last we were ready. We inspected each other approvingly.

'I like the effect of that chain belt round your neck.'

'Do you? I love the tassels down your skirt.'

We eyed our reflections, side by side, in the hall mirror.

'Is that the doorbell?'

'Phew!' said Tom, standing in the doorway with his sports jacket and sailing-red face. And then added valiantly, 'Hey, just look at this! You girls certainly have showed us up.'

We certainly had. They were coming for a nice cosy evening. A jolly foursome in a little bistro round the corner. The first thing I noticed about Tom's friend was his tie because of its extreme regimental neatness and its extraordinarily discreet pattern. Hardly a pattern at all. I couldn't help picturing with some misgivings our own scarlet rags and tatters. I smiled alluringly.

'Well,' said Jenny, just a little embarrassed. 'We thought we should make an effort. Pike, this is April.'

'Shake on it,' I said, meaning our ghastly names. But he seemed to take me seriously and we hooked hands in an energetic manner. Pike was dark with smooth straight hair and regular features of the sort which appeal to mothers. He had strawberry-coloured cheeks and dark patches where his beard wanted to spring forth. I imagined he was still rather embarrassed by it and carried an electric razor ready for the first signs of surfacing. However, he also had sharp blue eyes and was tall and rich-looking, so I forgave him the adolescent obsession.

'You're not working in London, are you?' I said as Jenny handed round a bottle of beaujolais and we looked for things to sit on.

'Thank God, no!' Pike leaned against the mantel with his arms across his chest while he spurned London in this easy way. I saw there was more to him than I had estimated. 'I can't see the point of cities. Can't live in them. Good for a visit and then I'm off.'

'Pike did agriculture at Reading,' said Tom not at all as if he was making a joke. My heart sank a little.

'Are you a farmer then?'

'Not the sort of farmer you're imagining.' He laughed heartily. I saw at once that as a girl I didn't merit any real explanation and resented it. 'And do *you* do anything?' He spoke boldly, though a little worried he was overstepping the mark.

'I'm a teacher.'

His face fell. He saw this outing had its drawbacks. But he was still determined to enjoy himself. He would generously overlook this failing on my part. 'I see. Well, well. Where are we off to?'

So the evening began.

Was it surprising I loved Lawrence?

Jenny didn't after all find it hard to ask Tom about a night-club because two glasses of wine did more for her than all my continual raids on the bottle did for me.

'I feel like dancing! Let's go dancing! Tom, I want to dance!' she shrieked and put her hand with the diamond engagement ring over his hand.

'Well, we can't go just anywhere,' said Tom.

'Don't be so uncreative!' she cried.

But it was Pike to the rescue. With a great air of mystery he reached into his jacket pocket and leant masterfully forward: 'I'm a member of Annabel's,' he announced, adding to slightly reduce the debonair image, 'my father made me a member.'

My thoughts were immediately of Lawrence. His place. His surroundings. His wife and her friends. Never far from the surface, he rose around me in all his ghoulish love and passionate attachment. Surely, he would be there? My skin went hot and I dazzled Pike with a toothy smile:

'How absolutely glorious!'

He looked at me with new interest. The wall between us which my profession as teacher had built in his mind seemed less impregnable. At least my heart was set on the right places.

Besides, possession of the ticket to Paradise made him supremely self-confident. A taxi stopped for him like a bird dropping to his gun and he undeniably squeezed my neck as he put me into it. Our evening had become suffused with a rosy glow.

I entered the hallowed halls with every tall man becoming Lawrence in his brown suit and floppy grey-yellow hair. My heart gasped in the Ladies at the possibility of

78

his wife at the washbasin.

'I've never been here before,' I said inanely to Jenny.

'Isn't it gorgeous!' Her eyes shone in innocent pleasure. 'I thought an outing would take you out of yourself.'

Inside it was so dark that I suddenly became worried. Would I know if it was him? But soon the golden lights grew in my face and, as we sat round our table, so efficiently captured by the excellent Pike, I could see exactly. No Lawrence.

Pike danced with me. The music was loud and rumbustious like children running down wooden floors, and it was very crowded.

No Lawrence. As if, I thought, that he came here every night or that the Gods should allow a guilty lady like me to have the ultimate guilty pleasure of seeing him in a public place where the lights are romantically low.

No Lawrence. Pike and I attempted to 'hit it off'. His phrase. But I kept forgetting he was a young man of no little sex appeal and peered hopefully past him. So the evening went on. And the rosy glow began to subside.

Pike and I danced round and I had my eyes shut, mostly because I was tired, when a hand reached down my back. I knew the hand too well. My blouse was thin and looped down my back. I opened my eyes. But the touch had fled.

'Shall we sit down?' mouthed Pike.

Now! I took no notice and assumed a sensuous slow two-step which involved him in a circular movement round the floor.

Now it had happened. Now he was here I found I was quite unprepared. My hands became clammy; my eyes crossed. Surely I hated him. Pike found himself suddenly brought to a standstill. Like an obedient horse he marked time. While my heart ballooned and subsided and popped into my mouth and got tangled in my stomach.

There he was. Lawrence, my lover, dancing with the most glamorous girl in the room (not even his wife) and between times running his fingers down my back. He looked at me now over her pointed shoulder, his eyes half-way between a blonde plait and a chin of beaten gold. He looked at me with eyes half-closed.

'Jolly good place this, isn't it?' shouted Pike suddenly. 'I'll tell my father what good taste he's got.'

Oh, no! Now! To so reveal himself and therefore me. I put my head on his shoulder and let him lead me away across the floor.

I sat crushed at our table. Not even the strength to torture myself with the sight of his wife.

And then he was coming. I saw him—still with the blonde plait—coming towards us.

'Oh!' Jenny spotted him with surprised blue eyes. 'That's my boss. I didn't think he'd be here.'

Because he's old. Because he's married. Because you don't think of him as a PLAYBOY with succulent lips and juicy mistresses.

So they would have the conversation:

'Hello, Mr Mann. Yes, this is my fiancé, Tom Lowell-Smith.'

'Mrs Lowell-Smith, eh?'

I didn't look at him. For the moment of glory, I looked at her—golden-swathed blonde goddess with haughty stare and bony wrists. She definitely wasn't his wife. A snake bracelet crawled up her ankle and she felt no need for words. I hated her far more than I loved him.

'And your flat-mate, isn't it? I believe we met before ...'

I writhed. I writhed. He bent over us and unwrinkled his eyes.

Schwep

602 – 2376

Mrs Eleanor
Curtis Billington
30 Addison Ave
W. 14

603 – 4318

THE
CHURCHILL

Mr. F. Z.

178 Mount St.

London, W.I

4th Floor
(London Sw and Andrews St)

'Yes,' said Jenny happily, 'I introduced you before. At last year's party. April Leventon.'

He wanted to shake my hand. I could see him longing to touch me. I pushed my hands firmly under the table. Beside me, Pike sat expectant, like a good dog waiting for an introduction.

'Pike,' I announced, imitating as much as possible the speechless hauteur of the blonde coiled plait. Who now unwound herself from a pillar and took Lawrence's arm:

'Darling,' she whispered. And they moved serenely on. At least I hadn't looked at him, let him touch me. At least I hadn't let him catch my eye. But how I looked at him as he left! My eyes bored like bullets into his back and then fixed like suction tentacles on hers.

'Pike has to get back to Basingstoke tonight.'

The rhyming couplet to end the sonnet. The epilogue. The epitaph ...

'Pike has to get back to Basingstoke tonight.' Of course he has. I knew what was required. Civilized, perfectly trained for outings like this, meetings like that, I knew when it was time to call it a day.

Jenny squeezed my arm: 'It took your mind off Anna going, didn't it? Wasn't it fun? Really.'

I stood up with a smile like a stone fountain's.

'Let's go then.'

'Go! Go! Go!' cried Pike, eagerly anticipating his return to the country.

'Gosh, it was expensive,' said Tom, more subdued.

'Oh, don't, darling!' cried Jenny.

I could feel the smile carved across my face like a dead grimace.

17

SICILY

It was completely silent in that room. The noise of the busy street outside must have been cut off by the shutters and the heavy drapes around the walls. Only Emmie's voice, whispering as silkily as her clothes slid off her body, spoke against my ear.

'Oh, I remember when I first saw you in London, in a night-club, with a young man, so nice looking, of whom you were so ashamed; so silent, you were all eyes . . . and then for the second time when you came to us in our house. I didn't know it would be you—Larry is so romantic about facts. He told me about your sister. Oh, yes, I know all about that. Whom you loved so much. Your Anna. I felt so sorry for you.' She stroked my forehead with her cool soft hand. 'And all evening you were so serious, so serious, so pale and sad. At that restaurant I even whispered to Larry as you gave in your coat, "Will she cry?" I asked him. And then suddenly,' her voice relived the surprise in a rising trill, 'and then suddenly, suddenly, no warning at all—how we all gasped! You laughed! Laughed in our faces!' And Emmie in delighted remembrance threw back her head onto my bare shoulder and laughed herself.

If there had been some other noise, some ordinary noise from the world outside, I might have been able to speak. Instead her body wrapped round me as I lay hypnotized.

'So gentle,' she cooed sweetly into my ear, her voice

changing once more to that infinitely mesmeric silken whisper. 'So passive, so innocent, so big, so soft, so white . . .'

The ss's hissed along my skin and tickled my ear drums. The darkness was so deep I didn't know whether my eyes were closed or open.

'Don't be afraid. You shouldn't be afraid. Look how small I am. Look how small my hand is.'

In front of my eyes pale strips of white appeared like far away ghostly figures. They rippled playfully and then it was dark again.

The fur of the rug gradually became warm from our bodies so that I felt we were lying in a gigantic downy bird's nest. My arms pressed along my back like folded wings.

'Lie quiet. Lie quiet,' Emmie sang.

18

ENGLAND

There is no death. There is a black swamp, fetid and steaming which holds some teetering on its elegant surface.

There was a green grass quivering pale like pampas in the wind which held up its head.

I am the black root, clawing my way with dirty fingernails along the stinking bed of the oily swamp. I am the black and hidden root to the silken pampas which waved its flowering head so bravely to the sunlight.

There is no death. I crawl along under the stinks and the smells, through undergrowth that tears my skin and slime that clogs my pores. My root, like a snout, pushes its way in remorseless corrupted movement.

There is no death. I am death. I drag down behind me the delicate grass till its fine stalk becomes all enmired with slime and the little blossoming fronds at the top are broken and crushed under the dark and the rot. The black root with its strong white flesh within drags down the little birth of sun and corrupts it in the night beneath.

There is no death. And she is dead. Black. Gone. Driven into the foul swamp. Lost forever. She is dead. Anna is dead. Her pale still face pressed into the foul ocean's pit. The swamp of filthy weeds where the sun is nothing.

I am death. My black swamp life is death. And now I have killed her.

It was as if I was trying to wash away her death in an endless flood of tears. They flowed out of my body with no restrictive hiccoughs or spasms. Whether I lay down or sat up, they poured out of my eyes.

Anna's plane crashed. There were no survivors. The telephone rang when we got back from the night-club—slouching around the flat, tired, drunk, with a bottle of Christmas brandy gulped crudely out of mugs. The telephone rang and I, trained like a gazelle to its merest quiver, hurdled Pike's outstretched legs to reach it first.

'229. 1001,' I whispered seductively, with my back turned to hide my intensity, and yet quite ready to rejoice in the conspiracy—I must remember not to call Lawrence by name—'Lawrence, my darling! How could I doubt you?' The death in the night-club wiped out immediately. He loved me. He loved me. I gripped the receiver with a delicate lover's smile.

I was gripping the receiver so hard that they had to force my fingers open one by one. Almost immediately my tears began to fall. And it was when Tom thoughtfully pressed on me the bottle of brandy that they increased to an uncontrollable flood. My memory of that time is entirely of water. Perhaps I hoped to drown myself also.

Yet, in a very short time they had become a hypocrisy. For I knew I could stop them when I wanted to. When I was ready. I knew I was crying more for myself than for Anna.

I lay in my bedroom in Dorset where Pike had driven me. Efficient Pike with his Annabel's card tucked securely into his inside pocket. I remember at the end of the journey thanking him politely for a good evening out and his enormous embarrassment.

85

The house was filled with lights which hurt my eyes. My father and mother sat upright in the drawing-room.

At first my mother and I fell into each other's arms. We hugged each other; she to find comfort in the living.

'My darling, we must pray together . . .'

And I . . . I did not say anything. I continued to cry. I thought, however, that Anna had died while Lawrence and I were making love.

My mother held me close, wetting her bosom and throat with my tears. 'She was so good,' she said, 'so happy.'

I thought with cold clarity that my future had died without my knowing it as I invited Lawrence to plunge on top of me.

'So perfect. So sweet . . .'

My tears poured over us both in a cool stream.

'Why should she die? We must pray together,' said my mother.

In the night I could hear my mother and father talking and weeping together. I cried silently.

And then it happened. On the fifth morning I woke up to find the sun spattering through my flower-patterned curtains and I did not begin to cry. I walked dry-eyed past the piece of lawn where Anna had particularly liked to sun-bathe; I opened a newspaper and discovered the print remained level; I ate hungrily.

And now we no longer found any consolation in each other, my mother and I. Our emotions disappeared underground. She no longer talked about Anna in front of me as I no longer cried in front of her. I put on a pair of earrings at dinner.

Two more days passed and it seemed to me that the empty vacuum we lived in now would go on for ever.

As if it had always been like this and always would be. My father went up to London and my mother and I passed the whole day without speaking a word to each other.

When my father returned he had arranged for them to go to Australia for the funeral. I was not expected to accompany them. My silence and composure had convinced them it would be best for me to return to my normal life in London.

I tried to speak: 'Would it be possible for me ...'

'Oh, darling,' said my mother, 'do you really want to? All that travelling.' She sat in bed with the breakfast tray pushed efficiently to the end of the bed. 'In term-time. It will only be a simple ceremony. Think of the expense. Do you really want to?'

Her practicality shocked me. I could not use my reason, could not show my feelings.

Father took me into his study. He patted my arm, and we both looked out of the window as he spoke.

'I think your mother will find it less of a strain if she doesn't have to worry about you as well, April. She is very brave and we don't want her to break down.'

I tried to speak again, 'Couldn't I do ... ?'

The gardener appeared outside the window pushing the large lawn mower. He bent to start up the motor.

'Better stay here ...' said my father hurriedly, anticipating the noise of the mower which quickly filled the room. I got up to go.

'Of course it's up to you,' father shouted suddenly above the noise. 'I'll certainly pay your fare.'

So they left without me. The two of them together; dressed in black.

She was dead, I told myself. Why should I go to Australia? She hadn't known it herself. I would mourn her where she had lived. So I went back to London. I considered on the train up from Dorset going to see her house, touching the chair she had lounged across, running my fingers along the empty cork notice board, taking a solitary walk through the straggly garden. But I didn't. I had the good excuse that the house was already occupied by tenants. But the real reason was that I had no desire to recreate Anna.

So instead I lay on my bed in the flat and pictured my parents together in black procession behind a black-tasselled coffin, while I was alone.

Then the tears started again, more noisily now—demanding sympathy and attention. Jenny made me hot drinks and sat with me. I seemed inconsolable to her. I cried in the bathroom, in my bed, till I would have had to change the whole bed to make it dry again. But I knew it was only the final protest. Merely a formality now. I had already made up my mind.

On the third evening after I arrived back in London, Jenny came up to my room. She looked worried:

'This man who keeps calling and you won't speak to, he's calling again.'

So I went down.

'My poor darling. I understand. What she was, is, to you. The love you had pouring out towards her, stopped, turned back on itself, all dammed up and turned to tears.'

How he loved emotions. He would drink my tears as if they were wine and then roll himself in them like a dog playing in a puddle. 'My darling. My beautiful love. Please come to me. Julia is away. You can come here. My darling.'

How he lowered my despair and yet became part of it. I was overwhelmed at once.

'I'll pick you up,' he said. 'Pack for a couple of nights. I want to help you. I love you.'

I don't think he had ever said that to me before. It took my sister's death.

'I'm going away,' I said to Jenny. She looked at me sorrowfully, trying again to cross the barriers of my swollen face and eternal tears.

'When people die,' she tried slowly, dutifully, 'they aren't unhappy. If you believe in,' even she hesitated at the word, 'if you believe in God and a life after, you've got to believe they're happy. Oh, April!' She wailed for I had begun to cry again. And then I stopped.

'God!' I shouted furiously. 'Do you think I believe in God after this? Do you think I'm smug enough to cosily say ah, well, she's happy now, where she is, up there with bouncy clouds. Do you think I believe in God? Who does this? I don't! I don't! I don't! You can believe in Him if you like because you're a silly little fool, but I won't!' I fled upstairs and rammed a nightdress into a bag. The most inappropriate of items. I hiccoughed over a hysterical burst of laughter.

Jenny followed me. I gulped and cried, making my sobs as loud as they wanted to be. I put my hands into my eyes and rubbed till they hurt. I zipped up the bag so that a corner of nightdress stuck out and tried to get past Jenny.

Her face was round and worried in the doorway.

'Get out of my way!' I shrieked. I thought she must have recognized Lawrence's voice. I increased my wails and sobs. 'You have your God, then stick to him, but don't bring him to me! Not now!'

But she didn't try to stop me nor mention Lawrence. I could see her mind was on the telephone and wondering

89

who she could ring. I could see she wanted Tom. Well, I wanted Lawrence.

'I'll be away two days!' I screamed, surprising Jenny with my rationality.

The moment I reached the street my tears stopped. How could I explain to her what I felt? The mixture. The reason and the emotion. Besides, whatever I said, she would sympathetically understand as bursting from the passion of the moment. If I said I was running away with Lawrence, she would have been sympathetic with disbelief. Who had shouted against God? Who had called her a silly little fool? She couldn't hear things like that. I watched Lawrence drive carefully up in his well-washed car and decided she was right: I hadn't shouted things like that. Not me. Soft and gentle. Weak and romantic.

'I wanted to see you. I wanted to see you so much.' I was in the car before it had stopped.

'Of course, of course.'

I huddled into his arms like Baby Bunting and for once he acted the role of father till his hand came closer to my breast and more conscious. I sighed and felt the tears drain away into the tension he drew through my body.

'What a sigh! What a sigh!' Keeping his left arm round me, he started up the engine again. 'I was fibbing,' he said. 'We can't go home. Julia's there. But I've told her I've got to see someone—a client, she knows . . .'

I didn't listen. 'Is it the weekend?' I cried quietly into his coat.

'Saturday.' With the voice of conviction. 'You haven't been at school, have you? I went there yesterday.'

'No. They let me off for the funeral.'

'And you didn't go to the funeral either. My brave

darling. To me you're always happy. Don't be sad any more. She's dead.'

Everyone could use words but me. My mother said, 'She died with her children, not for one moment alone.' My father said, 'There was no warning, nothing. She would have known nothing.' Jenny talked about God and happiness and now Lawrence, too. I was the only one who stayed silent, who cried noisily but said nothing.

Drearily, I sat up from his lap. It was a brilliant sunny day. We were driving through Regent's Park and since it was Saturday afternoon, the people and the flowers were competing for attention; and the ice cream vans and the man with balloons; and then the zoo with its entrance crushed with cars and children and prams. I wound down my window and the rich smell of the animals came through it all to me. I thought dazedly I could hear them bellowing and braying.

'You bring such joy to me,' Lawrence was saying: 'Such happiness. You have so much to give. Don't become sad like everyone else. You have such spirit, such dashing gladness. Don't give it up.'

Euston Road—we had passed through the park—was wide and thick with gleaming cars. My eyelids were heavy with the old dried-up tears and my face was too smooth and soft but my body, centred securely on the white leather seat, listened to Lawrence's hymn of praise. How could I help myself?

'When I see you, I live again. When I touch you, I feel again. You're my life, my hope and my love!'

'Where are we going? Where are we going?' I murmured submissively.

'To a friend's house in Islington.'

91

19

SICILY

Later Emmie lit a moss green candle as fat as a fist and dressed me again. Afterwards she dressed herself, taking down a new white linen dress which hung on the back of the door.

'Now we will walk a little,' she said. She combed her hair on to the top of her head so that her prominent bones dominated her face and then attached to it a false blonde plait. She screwed pearl earrings like small milky eggs into her ears and took my hand. I felt her coolness against my heat. My hair was in tangles down my back.

'I will make your eyes open wide as before I closed them.'

The streets were cooler now but fuller than ever with pedestrians. The girls' hair swept cleanly from their faces.

'*Buon giorno*,' Emmie said to a woman looking into a lingerie shop window, which shimmered with pale embroidered silk. I wanted to look too, but Emmie turned down a side street and then from another to another. I was half running. She didn't wait for me, but I followed doggedly.

Now the smart shops were replaced by low houses with divided doors like stables for horses. Old women and men sat outside on straw-seated chairs. Children played in the dusty cobbled street. I rubbed my eyes. The brilliantly lit poverty was in such contrast to the gloomy magnificence of Emmie's home. Washing trailed in sun-baked pallor above our heads. I was embarrassed and tried not to look through the open doors into the dingy rooms. Even so I couldn't help seeing the vast iron bedsteads that in most cases filled the single rooms. Occasionally a figure lay on one rolled up like a bolster. But Emmie did not mean us to stop and look. She walked unhesitatingly with a graceful healthy stride down the centre of the street. It was perfectly straight and only when she reached the very end did she stop and look for me. By then a long troupe of ragged children had collected behind us. They stopped when we stopped and gathered closer. Emmie seemed aware of them for the first time. Her smooth rocket-like height made an extraordinary contrast to their short dark limbs. 'Turisti!' they shrieked. 'Turisti! Dollars! Dollars! Pleeze!' Emmie bent down slightly; her brow was as clear and serene as ever. She pushed the white handbag to her elbow: 'Andate via! Maleducati! Va' a morir' ammazzato.'

She hissed out the words with such sudden icy distaste that they immediately backed away in fright and retreated to a safe distance. Only a few of the very brave cat-called their defiance. An old lady appearing at the door of her house looked out to see what was causing the noise. When she saw us she hurried back again, making the sign of the cross.

Emmie smiled in triumph first at them and then at me: 'An exhilarating walk, don't you think? After such a very lazy afternoon. Well now, I must return you to your master.' She sighed. 'And me to mine.' She took my arm in open comradely fashion. 'It has been nice, has it not? An experience, perhaps, for you?' She took my fingers and crossed them one over the other: 'It is horrid to be alone.'

20

ENGLAND

I am a black-hearted bird with gleaming purple plumage. By scarlet streamers I drag death behind me. My eyes close into hard buds with the warmth of the sun and flower wide in the night's cold.

Once I was a white lily with a golden heart, then I spread my downy petals to the sun and bowed my head respectfully to the night.

I am a black soul dragging death like a corpse behind me.

I am a plumed bird with feathers of gleaming purple, iridescent with silver blue and sharpest green. Through my beak runs a silver bit. Behind a silver curb. Across my back lie supple reins of skin and blood. I am driven.

The driver stands in the sky behind me and urges me forward. Forward, forward, through the winds and the massing clouds. I shiver to his hands on the reins and my back ripples with changing colours as if a wind blows on an inland sea.

When I swoop, curl and land, when the black charioteer calls me stop, then it is night. The ice-cold stars and moon light up my brilliance further.

I am no longer a bird. As I land the feathers part and ripple away from my back. Fall glittering like leaves from an autumn tree.

I am marble. I am a marble statue. I am placed and admired against black silhouetted trees. I am marble,

94

carved by my master. Created into slavery and unveiled to the world. The world gazes. They gaze. Stand back. Put out fingers and pop their eyes. Tongues waggle and talk around me. Touch my ice-cold wall with fingers soft like toffee.

I am marble. I am dead. For death has entered into my life.

'You'll like Emmie,' said Lawrence as we passed the Angel Islington and turned down a side street. 'She's to say the least unconventional.'

I sat back in the seat, my eyes half-closed. I was exhausted with crying. 'What about her husband?' I asked. As if he took me to see his friends every day. It had never happened before.

'He's Italian. Enrico. They're going off to Rome after dinner. That's why we can borrow their house.'

'Oh. I see.' I saw they were jet-setting away and wouldn't talk or only between planes when no one listened anyway. 'Who's in London now?' 'Oh, Larry with some young girl.' 'Larry? Ah. Isn't that our flight number?' 'Is Larry that publisher man?' Not real friends at all. He couldn't introduce me to real people. He wouldn't ever introduce me to real friends.

'Pretty square, isn't it?' We had turned off the side street of small pink and white houses into a wide grey square of grey mansions.

'Here we are.' We parked. And as we walked towards the house Lawrence took my arm and I thought greedily, We will be together in a house not his wife's.

The door which was stripped wood, not yet painted, was open.

'Oh, God! What a shambles! Darling! Darling!' a woman's voice shouted from the hall. Not to us. Lawrence advanced and I hung back. The woman had short boyish blonde hair and an elegant pointed face; she wore a long emerald green kimono; her feet were bare and she waved a cigarette at the end of a thin wrist. She seemed to be looking for something. Her search discovered Lawrence.

'Darling!' And then she called back to the other darling: 'Darling, Larry's here. It's ludicrous. I've been looking for an ashtray for simply hours and when you look at the state of the floor it would appear cuckoo.' She sang out the words like the herald of spring—tinged, however, with an un-English whistle and then flung her arms round Lawrence with belated impetuosity: 'So lovely of you to come, with all this mess! We shall go out and have a really splendiferous farewell dinner, yes?' Her voice became unmistakably Italian and intimate. I remembered she was supposed to be English.

'Enrico, my dear, is in the foulest mood. But then always when we move ...' Her voice drifted away and I wondered whether I should leave. I took a shuffling step and my feet caught an old piece of newspaper—the floor was laid with newspapers. The kimono spread wide and descended on me.

'April, Emmie.' Lawrence hastily introduced us. I stood fixedly. Hating the moment.

'But we've met. I'm sure of it.' Emmie surveyed me with her head on her hand and I was reminded. So was she.

'I know.' She pointed her cigarette at me like a gun and her eyes narrowed.

'At the night-club, eh?' She looked at my dazed stupid face and smiled, 'With the long blonde plait and the curling snakes.' And flinging her arms above her head she acted a sinuous snake dance.

'But you didn't talk there,' I said stupidly.

'Ha! Ha! Never at night-clubs. It is not chic.' She rolled her eyes and added matter-of-factly, 'Besides, the music's so loud that it would be quite exhausting.'

'Stop showing off, snake.' A very correct English voice came from under the stairs and embodied itself into a dark-faced man in impeccable English worsted.

'Enrico!' exclaimed Lawrence. 'Emmie says you're in a terrible mood.' They clapped each other's arms amicably.

'That's just to divert you from her own chaos. Are you sure you really want to stay here? In this pig-sty?'

Again I was anonymous. My eyes weighed in my head like marble balls.

'This is April,' said Lawrence baldly, and I saw without surprise Enrico's disappointment.

'So nice to meet you,' he said and put a hand across my shoulder. 'How about a drink?'

We sat in a circle with our drinks. In the tall partly furnished drawing-room. It had white shutters, a sofa, a judge's chair with red velvet seat and a pouffe. I sat on the pouffe with a green goblet of wine. Lawrence and Emmie sat on the sofa; and Enrico presided in the chair.

'Let the defendant come forward,' proclaimed Lawrence.

'I vote that the case in question is dinner,' said Emmie swinging a leg.

'Motion carried!' cried Enrico, slapping the arm of his chair.

I said nothing. I looked at Lawrence so agreeably, elegantly at home, and couldn't understand his passion for me. I looked at Emmie and Enrico and couldn't understand them at all. I thought with longing of my school and my forty-two children. There was a name and a face for me if I chose to take it. Teacher. 'Miss! Miss!'

After dinner I looked at Lawrence again. He was sitting across from me drinking his wine and laughing with Enrico.

'But your book, Enrico. Your book,' he was saying. 'How can I go on putting your name on expenses if you never write it?'

'But my dear Lawrence! You have yet to convince me you are serious. For when I sit down to think, one thought emerges: Another book on Italian houses? No! Impossible! So I throw up my hands.'

'And jump into an aeroplane!' cried Emmie.

The restaurant they chose was small and hot and crowded and I didn't feel like eating and I didn't feel like talking, so I continued to watch Lawrence. He began conversations and didn't finish them. He introduced a subject like a girl blushingly by the hand and then sat back smiling to watch her progress. If it seemed to flag a little, he would give a little pat to send it on and then relax once more. He sat back continuously. Physically. He slouched in his chair, trying to cross his legs where there was a table or reach them out where there was a leg. He was like an animal who had only just been trained to table. I thought of him walking round the flat naked and understood why he did it. He seemed uneasy in clothes. He spilled vichyssoise on his tie and a button came open on his shirt. Sometimes he looked at me. With his shiny brown eyes. Then I would look away embarrassed at their frankness. Rich mahogany eyes saying, 'Tonight we will be alone; tonight we make love; how we will make love!'

I looked nervously at Enrico; at Emmie. They had

started arguing about suitcases:

'A suit crushed or not is still a suit. But a crushed dress is a nothing!' Emmie appealed to Lawrence. 'Isn't that so? Shouldn't I have the hanger case?'

'Darling snake! Pack nothing. Carry it all on hangers. That way nothing will be crushed.' He hadn't taken his dark gaze from me. 'But why clothes anyway? Surely you just peel off your skin and reveal a gorgeous new set of silk spots and squirls?'

Emmie flung back her head so that it rested on the leather seat behind her.

'But brilliant!' She leant forward again and tapped Enrico on the forehead: 'In here, sweetest, there are no brains. No, no, no brains.'

I laughed suddenly, loudly and as if on cue the dinner was ended.

'When you laugh you are like Medea,' Lawrence whispered into my ear as we left the restaurant.

I mustn't laugh, I thought, or I shall cry again for my emotions are protected by only the thinnest layer of top soil.

The suitcases, it transpired, were at the Hilton. Emmie took Lawrence's face in her hands:

'Don't forget, my wicked publisher, that we expect you in Rome.'

'Old men and elephants never forget,' said Lawrence kissing her lips.

'And Palermo also,' said Enrico managing to make it sound as English as Surbiton.

'And April as well.'

They said farewell to me. Whose only sound had been the final laugh.

'Ah, *mi' amore*,' said Lawrence as they left and he

99

clasped my hands together in his. 'So silent, so pure like a pure white dove until suddenly she laughs.' He leant forward and ran his fingers round my eyes: 'Big eyes, big eyes. Look at me. Don't cry. Look at me wide open like you do when I love you.'

We walked back to the house and I didn't cry. I couldn't speak but I didn't cry. Again I was looking at him. With me he became different; less sure of himself and yet more dominating. He walked with longer steps and talked in round trailing sentences. He was proud and wary. He was like a cat with a mouse in its mouth.

The front door to the house was still open.

'There's sure to be a stunning bed with Emmie involved,' said Lawrence as if joking. 'They admired you tremendously.'

I remembered my jealousy in the night-club.

'Have you known Emmie long?'

'I believe the bedroom's at the top somewhere. Emmie?' He turned round at the stairs. He had caught my inflection. 'Too long to be embarrassed by questions like that,' he said, then proceeding phlegmatically upwards. 'Through three husbands—one of which was my stepbrother.'

I knew nothing of his life. I had too much pride to question him. I was humiliated and subject again. I stopped looking at him.

Anyway, we had reached the bedroom.

'Don't think so much, my darling.' He sat me on the bed. There was just a bed in the room. But bed enough for four. And a view through the windows of a sky as black as treacle. There was no light in the room.

'You wear no jewellery,' he said as he undid the zip at the front of my dress. I always felt like a tart when he undid that zip. Which he knew and liked.

'I haven't got any,' I said and managed to smile. 'I was given a ring for my twenty-first birthday, but it fell into the lavatory and sank without trace.'

Lawrence didn't like that sort of remark. It didn't suit his romantic image of me. He encircled my forefinger with his own fingers.

'Julia can't wear our wedding ring,' he said. 'She's allergic to metal.'

'Why don't you ask her if I can borrow it then?' I was sharp with dislike. But he would not notice it. Make note of it. I was out of my dress now and he was taking off his own clothes. Usually I watched mesmerized as his shirt, trousers, pants came off. That night I took off my own underclothes and carefully folded them under the bed. He liked to take them off and gloat over my skin where a strap had drawn a red line or where the day had left a blue bruise. But I had taken my underclothes off myself.

There was a flicker of freedom. Somewhere inside me. I lay back on the bed like an empty tomb waiting for the body.

21

SICILY

'Off where?' I asked Lawrence brusquely when I got back to the hotel. In the evening light he lay in his bed with the satisfaction of sleep still weighting his limbs.

'Ah,' he snorted, scrabbling for his watch on the bedside table.

'Had a good time?'

I have abandoned London, I told myself, where I never have good times. Emmie had given me what she had given Lawrence. I should be happy in the equality of it.

'Where are we going tomorrow?' I asked him again.

Where? It wasn't a 'where' with Lawrence. He knew the circuit, the Sicilian circuit of towns with cathedral piazza, drinking Stregas at a silver-rimmed table with the taste of olive oil lingering from supper. He knew already the early mornings at yellow temples, the long pot-holed roads through cornfields (Sicily—'the granary of Rome') or hot barren mountains. Segesta, Castelvetrano, Selinunte, Agrigento, Gela, Piazza Armerina, Syracuse, Catania, Taormina ... He knew Sicily without having been there. For him, it was more a tour of the Jolly Hotels; for he knew, too, how they strung—first class assured standard—round the island. The piazzas, the churches, the temples, the picturesque harbours were for me. A lollipop handed to me dutifully. Salving his glimmering conscience; expanding my mind as he buried his own.

I was his lollipop.

Love? I didn't look for it. I didn't care. No comfort from him. Only his need and my obsession.

We didn't know each other when we drove away from our first Jolly Hotel—bright sunny morning, two peaches from our breakfast on my lap.

'Selinunte by lunch?' suggested Lawrence. What did he feel? Was he happy?

22

ENGLAND

On Monday I went back to school. I was pale and exhausted from my weekend of love. My hands shook and
the powder wouldn't stay on my shiny nose. When I
came into the teachers' room, there was a silence and
then a bustle of activity. My shocked condition was all
too obvious. Mrs Smith handed me a cup of tea and patted
my hand.

'That's right. Pick up the reins again. But don't overdo
it now.'

I would like to have been hugged by her. But her
warmth was for the younger sister, the little teacher, the
good girl. Not the lover, the anarchist, still smelling of
adultery. I turned away to hang up my coat and saw
John's face.

'Hello, John!' I said. His emotions were so great that
he couldn't speak. He looked at me as if I was drowning.

'It's all right,' I said, trying to comfort him. And since
the bell rang he didn't reply. My voice which had been
choked recovered itself and I sang the morning hymn with
wide-open eyes. It was 'All Things Bright and Beautiful'.

The morning was grey and the children stretched out on
the parquet like a game waiting to be played. I felt quiet
and remote from them. I looked down at my hands and
they had stopped shaking.

In the classroom it was the same. Rows of solemn
torsoes sat behind their cube desks. I wondered they had

ever overwhelmed me. I realized they had been told I was suffering and yet the difference was in me not in them.

At lunchtime I let one of the docile sweeter-than-honey-girls carry my books to the teachers' room. I was amused by her self-importance and sober dedicated face. Her task finished, she poised herself at the door and enunciated clearly, 'Mummy says you're more to be pitied than a dog.' At which she tripped lightly away, secure in the knowledge of consolation well-delivered.

I would have smiled, except once again I caught John's anguished face.

'Shall we have lunch?' I said instead.

'Would you like to? Oh, yes.'

We went to a pub. I ate a large sausage on a stick and the fat ran down my fingers. I was drinking a gin and tonic.

'Please talk about it if it helps,' John said, crooking up his arm to get his small mouth at the beer. I, who had been thinking of nothing, replied as best I could.

'No. It was just so sudden.' I was struck by the lethargy which sadness and sympathy produce in people. We were like a couple in slow motion. I looked round and as I thought everyone else was drinking and talking and shouting and eating and laughing and grabbing at twice our speed, I bit up the remains of my sausage very quickly and turned to John.

'Let's go,' I cried. I marched out of the pub, arms swinging, head thrown forward with energetic determination. 'Life's great!' I shouted. John ran to catch up with me.

'I think you should talk about it—not run away from it,' he panted out beside me, the physical action apparently making him more bold. 'Your sister after all died suddenly without pain in the midst of her happiness. It is yourself you should feel sorry for. Don't be so brave. Talk about it.'

But to whom should I talk? To him? To the boy teacher and idealist sprinting at my side? To the evangelist, wallowing in his own repressed emotions? To him? Or to my parents, perhaps? Who produced Anna and myself in the same loving—I hope loving—way and now have only me. But I had never talked to them. How could I start then with such a big venture?

Then should I talk to the man I love? Of course I should. If I loved him. Who is he to feel a sister's death? Already it has become part of his dark romantic vision of me. Made me more appealing, my silence and hidden depths deeper. If I could talk to him; if I could talk to him I wouldn't be with him, I would shout and scream at him and cry out adulterer! And I don't love you! And I hate you!

'Don't run like this. You'll get run over.' John who had managed to come level with me grabbed hold of my arm. He held me swaying on the edge of one of the side streets I had been flinging myself across. He looked at me sadly, 'Try not to be so upset.'

Upset! What puny words he used for me. We walked back to school soberly. John eyed me sideways making obscure remarks about the people we passed on the pavement. He was afraid I would break out again.

'I'm afraid we're going to be late.' He looked serious as we approached school.

'It's just the play for mine.'

He taught the eleven-year-olds, the workers. The examtakers. I wanted to be a dedicated teacher. I wanted to lose myself in my children.

'Thank you for lunch, John,' I said calmly outside my classroom. My calmness had never left me. Only my body had filled with energy. 'Perhaps you're right about talking out things.'

The children had already pushed back the tables and were locked in excited hierarchic groups. They were ready to pounce the moment I came through the door and yet I came quietly into the room and was at my own desk before they spotted me.

'Miss! Miss! Miss!' The best actor group flung themselves towards me now with the vigour of the cheated.

'Miss!' cried Lauren, a dashing red-head whom I rather admired for never offering to wash out the sink, clean the board or other girlish activities. 'Miss! My mum says she'll make me a pink satin costume out of a lovely old nightdress she's got if you make me the princess!'

'But there isn't a princess in the play, Lauren.'

'See! Silly! I told you so.' An unpleasant child whose glasses and rolling stomach put her straight out of the princess category, gloated vociferously. 'My mother wears pyjamas!' she continued self-righteously.

'With what she's got, she'd have to,' shouted a lascivious voice.

'Wheeee, whoooo ... Pop ... Pop ...'

'Fatty Judy's mum's a man. Fatty Judy's mum's a man.'

They found it easy enough to say what they thought ...

'Silence, please! And I'll tell you your parts.'

The play was *Othello* adapted by myself, because one of the West Indian boys was a particularly good actor. Lauren's instinct had been right. Her mother's nightie would be a great addition to Desdemona.

We would begin, I decided, with the murder scene. It was sure to captivate my actors.

'Sheet number six. The cast list's at the top. Lauren, you're in bed.'

'Upstairs and downstairs in her mummy's nightie,' a sly voice mocked from the basins.

'On the floor, miss?' said Lauren, meekly lying herself down. Carefully folding her skirt round her legs.

'Put out the light!' cried Othello.

'Miss! Miss! Shall I pull the curtains? He said turn off the light, but as it's day shall I draw the curtains?'

' "Thou art to die!" ' shrieked Othello.

Too late I saw his intentions. Suddenly he had thrown himself on the brave Desdemona and was clasping his black hands round her pink throat.

'Miss! Miss! Miss! He's killing her!' the eager audience chorused.

'Owwww! You're hurting me!' screeched Lauren, pushing him off her with furious strength, and scrambling to her feet.

'I saw Lauren's knickers!' chanted a disappointed rival.

'Enter Emilia,' I said emphatically.

'But I haven't killed her yet. It says here ...' Othello studied the print self-righteously, 'it says here "smothers her with cushion".'

'Wring her neck like a chicken and see if she walks,' egged on Othello's friends.

'We'll do the murder scene when you're feeling more civilized,' I said severely. 'Enter Emilia.'

A small girl whose asthmatic hunch won her elderly roles came quavering, heavily over-acting on the left.

' "Villainy. Villainy. Villainy," ' she whispered hoarsely.

'Miss! She croaks like an old frog!' The audience at the back sat on a table and swung their legs derisively.

108

Baulked of more murder, they were in no mood for old ladies.

'Speak out, Irene!' I ordered. 'A murder's just been committed. Your young and beautiful mistress is lying smothered on the floor, that is, the bed.'

Lauren who had resumed her wan pose on the floor began to giggle.

'There she lies—pale as monumental alabaster. Would you not scream, shout out: "Villainy! Villainy! Villainy!"?' Irene looked up at me with big serious eyes. The room seemed to recede from me.

I went away and sat behind my desk. Villainy. Villainy. Villainy. My thoughts moved smoothly into their usual well-worn channels.

I decided to go and visit Lawrence when school finished. At work. I had never visited him at his office. I would pretend I was looking for Jenny. Perhaps the impersonal surroundings would make me speak out.

Laughter broke loudly round me. It crystallized into words.

' "Where is that viper? Bring the villain forth!" ' My chosen duke stood on a chair in mad gesticulation. The noise rose into a crescendo of high-pitched, bowdlerized Shakespeare.

I would enter, I thought, Lawrence's office with dignified calm.

23

SICILY

A boy's face, ... narrow and intent, ... at the exit of the
Jolly Hotel passed so close to my car window that it seemed
to press against the glass. I turned away sharply. I faced
Lawrence's profile. But I couldn't speak; Lawrence and
I didn't talk to each other. Yet he had come away with
me alone. I tried to comfort myself. He had left behind
Enrico—so much more interesting a companion than me.
He had left behind Emmie. He never questioned me. Why
did he never question me? Yet, indisputably, he was driv-
ing me—in a car that crooked his legs like a stork's.

I looked away from him. Around us the city spread into
an apparently endless rectangle of streets. It was much
bigger than I had expected. Foreign cities, I had thought,
were intimate areas where one strolled leisurely from
one view to another. It took us half an hour before I saw a
hot, dried, alien-looking mountain—beyond the cars, the
buses, the noise, the energy of any modern city.

'Eight o'clock in the morning seems to be Sicilian rush
hour,' I said.

But to Lawrence it was merely London—without a wife,
without child, without work; no responsibilities, except
just a little to this girl who satisfied his romantic sensu-
ality.

So Lawrence was not surprised by the traffic. He didn't
answer me. But I thought we must talk. So I said as we

passed through one last wide street before leaving the city:

'Isn't this where Danilo Dolci worked?' And as I spoke I saw more clearly the small and dirty homes on either side of us, spilling over the pavement—some like little cardboard boxes, some wigwams of corrugated iron. And all as close to each other as a pile of children's bricks, as higgledy-piggledy too, although the only colour came from the dirt and some washing, not very much washing, draped disconsolately on pieces of rubbish.

Our car travelled smoothly, blindly, through it all.

It made the street Emmie had led me through seem like the tourist attraction she had used it for. I blushed hotly at the memory and shame made my voice shrill:

'Look at them!' I exclaimed.

'You mustn't let your eyes destroy your sense of proportion. Far worse things are happening all over the world. Far more people are dying with far greater suffering. Here it's a problem in tens instead of thousands.'

'You're not even looking!' I grew hotter still.

'My darling, one can't look at everything. Besides, when you're as old and tired as I am you'd rather read about things than look at them. I've read about slum-living in Palermo. I can imagine it only too well.'

'But we're driving through it!' My eyes pricked with frustration.

'Not any more.' And indeed, in my fervour, I had not noticed we were now streaking along a wide grey road running between rich olive groves garlanding the rising mountains. There were few other cars and the sun had risen till it glittered across the dark crest of fir trees.

'Ah!' I sighed involuntarily and stretched my legs.

'There!' Lawrence smiled at himself or me in the mir-

III

ror. 'You see. It's easy to look beyond.' And again we fell into silence.

I had never noticed before how satanically his eyebrows lifted above his deep-set eyes. They were completely grey and the hairs met together in triumphant arches and then swept away to the side of his face with a fine flourish. I tried to imagine his face without them. In profile it would be all nose. His nostrils, too, now I noticed, were much bigger than I expected. And his hands on the steering-wheel were as wide and firm as cricketing gloves, except that smooth-folding layers of hair lay between the joint and the knuckle. I couldn't see the fingers, but I remembered how flat they were and round-ended.

The silence was filled now with the noise of the car. It could never be filled with words.

All male, Emmie had said. Something of her had entered me now. Something insinuating and silky. All male. Heavy. Burdening me with his weight. It was that I loved. And now the weight of the sun was added to it, rising, higher, hotter, and heavier, seeming to fill him with the expanse of its warmth, till I was squeezed down, battened, crushed.

And still he did not speak.

We were inland now with no wind to carry in the cool glassy ripples off the sea. Only the mountains, becoming all the time more exposed as the vineyards dropped lower down their slopes. Yellow, a sterile yellow, like sand, a sifting of dead nature, came up as if from underground and overtook the greens and browns. Just once I saw a few pink flowers suspended on a spidery scaffolding of green scrabble desultorily across the yellow. They were so little attached to the ground that the faintest whiff of breeze would have blown them into the sky and fragmented them like dry paper, confetti, before the sun.

But no breeze came. The day was as still as I.

'We must be near Selinunte,' said Lawrence casually as if breaking the silence of a moment, rather than an hour. 'This heat isn't very comfortable.'

The road began to climb. My wet back clung to the plastic car seat. And the yellow again became faintly tinged with brown and green. The road widened quite suddenly and some prickly greyish-coloured plants spiked through the ground on either side.

'In spring,' said Lawrence in a lazy reminiscent voice, 'they are covered in deep pink flowers like rosettes. They're oleander bushes. Their flowers are the colour of your cheeks when you blush.' He looked sideways at me across his nose, 'Or when you're hot like now, my darling.'

'Well, they're dead now.'

But a great explosion of sound swept across my words, filling the car and drowning my voice—at least to my own ears.

We had come to Segesta. And there were huge coaches roaring and revving, car doors swinging open on their hinges, with a hideous jangle of music pouring out from all their combined radios. And then people, straddling and striding across the car park and up a row of steep stone steps.

That was the way I saw the temple—led up to it by restless tourist paraphernalia. There it sat, solid and silent, with its great stone pillars the same yellow as the dead mountains we had passed.

The first crowd of people reached the base of the great pillars while the rest still straggled, zigzagging upwards. In their brilliantly coloured clothes, red and blue and green, they looked like flags strung out on the ground ready to be raised.

Lawrence drove the car to the shade of a gaunt tree above the car park.

'Well,' he said, 'here we are. Now we'll find out if you know the difference between a stylobate and a peristyle.'

'Let's wait till they've gone.'

'I suppose we couldn't make love in the car. I expect the Sicilians would lynch us.' He laughed.

I stared.

'Are those Sicilians?'

'He is.' An old man on a donkey tasselled and fringed with coloured cord, came out from behind us and passed into a field ahead. He looked away as he passed. He was thin and old.

'And those are, too.' He pointed below us to the car park where a swarm of little white cars like ants between the fat coaches overspilled with jumping chattering figures.

'They look like a herd of monkeys,' I said scornfully, for from a distance their arms seemed long and their legs disproportionately short and crooked. Besides they were cavorting in a haphazard fashion more like monkeys than men. 'What are they doing here? Not sightseeing anyway.'

'Oh yes, they are. We leave our New World to see their Old World and they come to their Old World to see the New World—us. A friend of Enrico's swopped one of his castles for a racing car, and then an earthquake shook the castle down. A most practical lot, Enrico's compatriots.'

'I had forgotten he was Sicilian.'

'He'll be delighted.'

I wondered if Lawrence really believed in the earthquake. He probably enjoyed the idea too much to allow any doubts. As Emmie had said he was a romantic about facts.

I watched the car park again where the noise and energy had increased to new heights. The coaches had formed themselves into a line and the boys, having fixed their cars in a racing semi-circle, were dancing off to meet the returning tourists. Down the hill the flag rolled up and with sudden extraordinary speed disappeared into the coaches. There was a noise like twenty-five jet bombers as coaches, cars, a scooter or two I hadn't noticed, all took off up the road. Then, suddenly, total silence.

Lawrence got out of the car and slammed the door.

'The boys went too,' I said, surprised.

'If you'd been on your own they wouldn't have. Are you missing young blood, my darling?'

We walked side by side up the smooth-cut steps and the sun was everywhere so that I could feel it even on my ankles and heels. When we reached the front colonnade of pillars Lawrence ran his warm fingers up my bare arm:

'This would be even better than the car.'

'We're being watched.'

In the centre of the temple a brown-skinned man, dressed in blue overalls with a white handkerchief knotted over his head, held upraised a bottle of wine and watched us. When he saw we were looking at him, he stared a moment longer and then tipped up the bottle for a drink so that it hid his face.

'Pillars have eyes,' said Lawrence desultorily, poking the ground with his sandals. He was wearing heavy buckled brown sandals. Some palish brown hairs covered his instep. I went over to see what the man was doing. We peered together into a rectangular trench.

'You see here the flower of Sicilian archaeology,' said Lawrence ironically.

The man now sat side-ways with his back against a pillar. A lizard ran out from his trench.

'Oh, look!' I cried.

Behind the temple a slow frieze of bent figures was moving across the land. They seemed to be picking something from a wild pricklish-looking plant and as they passed by us and out of sight, a harsh crescendo of voices rose and fell again. The workman with his bottle turned his head to watch them as they disappeared over the hillside and then turned back. He didn't speak. I sat down with a sudden content in the shade of a pillar.

'There must be a village nearby,' said Lawrence. 'Shall we go and see the amphitheatre now?'

'It's a very domestic temple, isn't it? Lived in.' My content was changing to exhilaration. High in the mountains as we were now, the air seemed lighter and sparkled with the unveiled sun.

We drove up a steep road to the theatre and half-way up we met the coaches and the cars and the scooters coming down. Lawrence stopped on the verge and they swept past us in wild Bacchanalian rout. I saw the face of the front coach driver. It was very dark and his eyes were egg-shaped and black. Behind him like a string of pale beads after the clasp swept a row of round flat faces, many of them, as if they had toothache, bound up in coloured scarves.

And then as before the silence came again and filled the empty space they had left. I saw the sea rushing into a hole in the sand. We stood side by side on the top of the amphitheatre, and my head was filled with sun and silence in a great burst of exultation. Like a child I wanted to shout, 'I'm the king of the castle!' I turned to include Lawrence in my glory. But he was not beside me any more.

'It's too hot to climb down.' His words hit the air dully, like a clapper hits a tied bell. He had moved a few yards away until he stood along the top of the curved rows of seats. The sun shone behind him so that I could only see his black silhouette and hear his dead, flat voice. Slow and lethargic killing my life. My heart seemed to multiply and beat painfully in face, arms, legs, body. It pushed me into action. I started to run, scrabbling and jumping, down the tiers of seats. My clutching fingers scraped on the stones, the thongs of my sandals tugged between my toes, my feet slipped on a running cascade of small pebbles, my head pounded and throbbed and the sky swam with scarlet and black blotches. I reached the bottom and crouched down shaking. But how good I felt. I told myself that. How alive! How free!

Slowly the black and red became mauve-tinged and green. Then faded into little foetal coils and squirls. I looked up.

The circular line of the theatre clipped neatly into the dark blue sky. I waited. But there was no movement. I looked again. There must be something. Some reaction. Some great responsive movement. I had to have it. The skyline was quite clean now.

He *had* moved. He had sat down. I saw him now. Where he had stood, now he was sitting; squatting like a black bird on the rim of the seats. If he saw me looking up at him he made no sign. Or perhaps his head was bent onto his knees. I could only see a black stone eagle.

We stayed for a long time like that under the blazing midday sun. Myself on the stage of the theatre, crouched down, sobbing with exhaustion and frustration. He at the top, unmoving. Apparently incapable of movement.

Eventually, when my body had become as still as his, I did what I knew I would when I saw him sitting there. I climbed slowly up the side of the seats and walked along the top. I sat down beside him.

24

ENGLAND

The girl who is me walks like a statue stepped off a pedestal. She holds herself stiffly and doesn't ask the way because she has only a few words in her mouth
I have only a few words. 'Villainy. Villainy. Villainy.' They echo in my vaulted mind.
The building is tall, smooth-faced and grey. Now the glass doors swing behind me cutting off the noisy, nosey world.
'Fifth floor. All the pretty girls go to the fifth floor.' There is a figure at a desk who speaks but I don't answer.
The purple cubicle ascends quietly, two girls opposite me have clacking mouths but their eyes are fixed and staring. Black-rimmed as if in mourning.
Black doors slide into themselves and we step out together, in a line of three, they wear brilliant shoes, square-toed, green and yellow.
I am pale. I am marble. I am old and decided.
'After you.'
'No, after you.'
They swish and duck through each other's arms and we have entered a red door. Around us the walls are red.
'Oh, yes, Jenny. Shall I buzz her?' My heart is white and breathless against the scarlet walls.

Lawrence's publishing house was in the middle of

London. I sat on the top of a bus, at the front, and felt glad it was empty. And when it thrust through the crowds of Oxford Street I was so high that I could look down as a spectator. There was a sad burden of summer feeling about people: limp dresses under sagging cardigans; frizzled perms from sea-side holidays; handbags fat and blown with the season's junk; stomachs swollen with self-indulgence in the sun or in compensation for the lack of sun. I looked at them from my superiority and tried just for a moment not to think of myself. But my superiority didn't allow me to be really diverted.

I left the bus at Oxford Circus and walked a little. But people were even more depressing on the same level.

Three boys passed with dangling plastic spiders, just bought from a pavement stand. They smiled at me and made the spiders dance:

'Cheer up! It may never happen!' cried one.

And I couldn't even smile. I thought of stopping for a drink but knew I would cling to the glass till Lawrence had left his office.

I stood in front of the glass-faced building and looked up. Two girls darted in past me. I followed their swiftness and gaiety like an old thrush behind two humming-birds. I pushed through the doors.

'Fifth floor. All the pretty girls go up to the fifth floor,' shouted the commissionaire at the desk as we passed him. I was surprised to be included.

Inside the lift the girls were talking:

'We swore publicity was a stepping stone.'

'To the literary side, I know.'

'And the pay doubles the moment you've got more up there than a pretty face. He said.'

'He didn't even say I had a pretty face.'

They started to laugh and the lift doors closed.

Thomas Hill. Publishers.

The three of us stepped towards the same door. I suddenly wondered how I looked and stopped for a moment to find my mirror.

'After you.'

'No, after you.' The girls having settled their priorities, bright eyes enquiring, held the door for me. Flustered, I went through. And we were encased in a scarlet mouth of walls. They chattered round a corner. Oh God! The receptionist was also enquiring. I had only pictured my presence in Lawrence's office. Not all this business. I gave my excuse for being there:

'I'm to see Jenny Cole, please.'

'Yes. Her office is just round the corner. Shall I buzz her?'

'No, no. I'll find it.' I went quickly round the corner. I had imagined there would be revealing names on office doors. But the doors were anonymous wood grain. There was only the corridor with a carpet, the scarlet walls; even the secretaries were hidden. I started to cry like a fool and a door popped open. One of the girls from the lift came springing towards me.

'Could you tell me where Mr Mann's office is?'

'I'm his secretary actually. Do you have an appointment?'

'Yes.'

She had chestnut hair tied back from her forehead in a yellow bow. She wore a sleeveless dress and her arms were sunburnt. She led me through the varnished door and her hair was just as shiny.

'Mr Mann...' She buzzed at her desk telephone. But I was bold now, tears flying from my eyes. Blindly I pushed through the door to his office. It was a cupboard. My face pressed against a coat and a shopping bag. The smell of leeks surrounded me. I started to laugh. I turned round and saw Lawrence come through a second door. I continued to laugh. So hard I had to put down my handbag and my eyes were wet again.

'Oh, it's my niece,' I heard him say sternly. 'It's quite late, Susan, why don't you go home now?'

'Is she all right?' Dubious voice as I giggled and cried.

'Just a bit hysterical. That's all.'

I stopped erupting and found I had been led into a green office with curtains and a sofa. Lawrence placed me into it and then sat on a low leather chair; he put his legs relaxedly on the desk but his face was sad.

I was seized with fear. Perhaps he would stop loving me. Perhaps he already had. He looked remote and distinguished and sad. The way I loved him most. I was so terrified at what I'd done that I couldn't speak.

'Perhaps we'd better stop meeting.' He put down his legs and half-covered his face with his hands. 'If it makes you so unhappy.'

'But it doesn't! It doesn't!' I cried. 'I love being with you.'

'Crying is not a sign of happiness.'

Oh God! I thought. He's doing it. He doesn't want me any more. He's found someone else. Gayer, more amenable.

'I'm just emotional,' I said, tears streaming down my face. 'It doesn't mean I'm unhappy. I'm only unhappy when I'm away from you.'

'I'm too old for you.' He sighed.

'No! No! No!' I pleaded desperately.

'You're so young. You care so much about things. I

don't want to hurt you.'

'Oh no! Oh no! You make me so happy!' I sobbed out the last word and choked to a standstill.

'I don't know,' he said in the same flat depressed voice which struck a miserable chord in me. 'I thought we could bring something to each other. But perhaps there's too much of a gulf between us.'

'We do! We can! Oh please!' I could think accusations. Yes, I could, but I couldn't watch him accuse himself. Please no, Lawrence. Don't say it. If he said he was married, there would be a marriage between us; it would be there always and everything would be over. Please, Lawrence! I had to get out. Go before he said it. I blew my nose. I had to be strong. He was slumped in his chair. Apparently uncaring if anyone came in and saw us. I loved him. How I loved him.

'I'm sorry,' I said. 'I just lost control. My sister, you see ... You know.' I used her easily, grabbing without guilt at the best excuse. I stood up, straight and strong. I stood up. 'Are you ... ? Lunch tomorrow?'

He looked at me. I tried to smile. He spoke sideways at me :

'I was going to ring you this evening. I had a plan. I know. Your sister ...' His voice trailed away and then picked up again. 'Something nice, I thought. But now I don't know.' He looked at me with drooping chocolate eyes. There was a pile of manuscripts on his desk which he flipped at with his fingers.

'What?' I said staring, fascinated at the blunt-ended fingers which had touched me so often.

'I have to go to Sicily. Stay with Enrico and Emmie for a day or two. I thought you might like to come.'

'But ... How could you ... ?'

'It would be term time. Julia couldn't come anyway. It would only be for a few days. But now, I'm not sure. For you.' Gloomily he pushed the manuscripts away.

'School term.'

The telephone rang. Mechanically, Lawrence lifted the receiver. I heard an operator say, '. . . long distance.' It was my chance to leave. To pretend this meeting had never happened.

'Yes . . . Yes . . .' Lawrence picked up a pen.

I must go gracefully. Happily. I blew him a kiss. Mouthed goodbye. Then he would ring. He would remember me young and gay and carefree. Just a little hysterical for a moment. Her sister died. Perhaps he would believe that. I smiled my way to the door. I turned. And he tapped the receiver and pointed to me. He would ring.

Triumphant, with a smile like a five-barred gate, I marched down the corridor. I swung my bag patronizingly at the empty receptionist's desk, I congratulated myself on my glorious happiness.

25

SICILY

We sat side by side on the top of the amphitheatre. We might have been tourists exhausted by our steep climb in the midday sun.

'I'm too old for you,' Lawrence said. His face, now that he turned towards me, was drawn into hard downward lines from brow to nose, from mouth to chin. His hair as if he had been running his fingers through it stood out in stiff waves. His own head had become a puppet's head, caricatured in *papier mâché*. His body below seemed bundled and useless as if only his clothes held it together.

Then slowly and sadly, as if more from habit than desire, he put an arm round me.

At first it hung loosely, weightlessly, and it gave no warmth. The fingers tickled my arm a little, but that was all. Gradually, very gradually, a hot weight seemed to grow along it. It became very heavy.

Lawrence shifted his feet and with his big fingers caught onto and held my shoulder.

'Well,' he said, 'we've certainly earned our lunch and a siesta.'

26

ENGLAND

Jenny and I sat opposite each other in our cosy little sitting-room. It was ten o'clock and we were sewing. We had been sewing all evening.

The idiotic balloon of good spirits I had created round myself on leaving Lawrence's office was stretching very thin.

Jenny was making a dress for herself and I was making a turban for Othello.

The balloon burst the moment I had sewn the last silk fold into place and attached a purple feather with a Woolworth's emerald brooch to the front. I tried to pretend I hadn't heard the pop.

'Look!' I held up the turban for Jenny's approval. It glittered beautifully and I could imagine how splendid it would be above Leon's black face.

'You are clever!' Jenny cried. 'My dress seems so dingy by comparison.'

'I'll make some coffee,' I said and, in an attempt to mock away my deflation, propped the turban on the top of my head. I shimmered into the kitchen. But the black smog, shot through with green, was waiting for me; the kettle's whistle was muffled, my hands bumped clumsily; my head was thick and unthinking. Lawrence had not rung. He had not telephoned his gay young innamorata.

'You can't put salt in the coffee.' Jenny was laughing

behind me. I poured the coffee down the sink silently and watched it bubble up again as the blocked drain spat it out.

'The sink doesn't take salt either.'

'Why is our drain always blocked?' cried Jenny gaily.

'Because we pour fat down it. And it coagulates.' Desultorily I poked the hole with a spoon handle.

'Oh, look out! That's my christening spoon.'

'Sorry.'

'It is squalid in here. How about doing some washing up?'

'We can't. The drain's blocked.' I sloped back to the sitting-room. I felt like a tired cow with head lowered and wavering slowly from side to side. 'Jenny?'

'Yes.' She took up her sewing comfortably.

'Have you ever been to Sicily?'

'No. Tom went. He says it's a violent place. He won't take me.'

'Oh, really? It's run for the tourists.'

'By the Mafia.'

'Poof! Old wives' tales!' I kicked our battered tin waste-paper basket. 'I could do with a bit of violence anyway. Horror. Violence. Death.'

'April!' Jenny was shocked. She looked away. Her thoughts shot vibrations at me.

'Anna. Anna. Anna. Your sister. Anna.' Little red wriggling sound waves. Like broken veins in broken legs. Smashed into the sea-bed.

'That's just the point,' I said, kicking the wastepaper basket again. 'Oh, you wouldn't understand.'

'No. I'm sorry . . .' We both watched her complete a long row of tacking stitches. Then she had an idea. 'Pike asked me about you the other day.'

'Pike?'

'Yes. I thought we might all have a weekend together.'

'Naughty. Naughty.' I wagged my finger at her. It was pink and obscene before my smoggy eyes.

'Not a dirty weekend.' She did a good imitation of Tom's hearty laugh. 'I meant staying at home.'

'To the pure all is pure.' My eyes fixed on a ladder in my stocking. I flexed my leg so it spread further.

'Well, at home it is. Pike's coming the weekend after next. My parents adore him.'

'That lets me out.' I scratched my ankle which had begun to itch maddeningly. Little animals were crawling under my skin.

'They have passionate conversations about sewage.'

'I was planning to make a knife for Othello.'

'He doesn't stab her.'

'Symbolically speaking.' I leaned my head defeatedly on my knees.

'You are in an odd mood,' said Jenny perceptively.

'I'm sorry.' I tried to clear the fog. 'I'd love to come to stay.' I got up with an immense effort of will. 'I'm going to have a bath.'

I did my best with the pine essence in the steaming bath. With the black night coming through my little private window. With my bed which I first made and then lay on. I even put some sordid underclothes to soak —defeated by the next creatively satisfying step as I looked in vain for the washing powder.

So I put the Othello turban back on my damp head and stared at myself in the bathroom mirror. My haughty nose evoked a Victorian dowager. Othello-like, I rolled my eyes. Better. I bared my teeth and snarled. A definite improvement. I pressed my nose flat against the glass. It

128

seemed to become fixed there and my breath misted over my image.

> ' "Therefore confess thee freely of thy sin;
> For to deny each article with oath
> Cannot remove, nor choke the strong conception
> That I do groan withal. Thou art to die." '

I whispered hoarsely, eyeball to eyeball.

'Thou art to die. Thou art to die. Thou art to die.' I made it more evil, more twisted. Yet how heartfelt! How pure! Oh, admirable Othello! With one sharp action cleaning out the poison in his clean soldier's life. 'Ugh! Grrrh! Aaaaggghh!' My face swam in front of me. The bathroom was as hot as Sicily. 'The great thing about Sicily is the sun. Tom got quite black when he went there.' I mimicked Jenny to myself.

'Thou art to die.'

I started to laugh and the laugh grew in a never-ending corkscrew. My head spun off it into blackness.

27

SICILY

We were staying at a Jolly Hotel in the flat plain town of Castelvetrano.

'Why are we staying here?' I asked disliking at once its ruler-straight streets, its stark signs of Birra Messina and its apparent lack of trees or piazzas or even churches.

'Because it's got a Jolly Hotel.' The building was new and unwelcoming. The foyer was dark with mahogany. Some men sat drinking at a bar. 'It's supposed to be the headquarters for the Mafia,' Lawrence laughed. 'Anyway, it's only our room that matters, isn't it, my darling? Or I'll even narrow that down further to the bed.'

The man behind the desk was big and tall. The big men of Sicily, I thought, seemed reserved to be hotel clerks.

'One night only, sir?' he said with a very good English accent and an un-Italian hauteur which seemed to imply that only a fool would book in for one night.

'Yes,' said Lawrence, unnoticing. It was about two-thirty, but the brilliant sun didn't reach us through the massive curtain of beads that hung across the door. And there seemed to be no windows.

'The lift is not in condition,' said the man behind the desk. 'You are on the fourth floor.'

'Send up a bottle of white wine and some *aqua minerale*,' said Lawrence, and he took my arm. We walked slowly up the stairs which had the same vaguely

Eastern carpet as the Jolly Hotel in Palermo. A very small man carrying our suitcases with unlikely ease darted ahead and unlocked our bedroom door with a flourish. It was pitch black. He scurried to the window and the blinds sprang open bringing back the stark glare of sunshine and a view of a tall partly constructed building. Around it lay the flat dry plain.

'Let's shut them again.' Lawrence flung himself on the bed furthest from the window.

'He's left the door open,' I said, going across to lock it and so I couldn't help hearing the lift come up and seeing a waiter step briskly out with a tray.

'Our drinks came up in the lift.' The waiter came in and after looking round vigilantly put them down.

'It's probably been mended.' Lawrence rolled towards me in an attitude of supplication. 'Give me to drink.'

'He's brought red wine.'

'Anything! Anything!'

The wine was the same dark brown colour as the varnished furniture which filled every space in the small room.

I gulped. And he gulped. We set down our glasses together and poured out more. I could feel my stomach at first contract and then loosen and relax. The heat of the day which before had lain uncomfortably on the surface of my skin now penetrated my whole body with a rich comforting glow.

I lay back on my bed and waited to make love.

28

ENGLAND

My face is black. It is a black silhouette against the brilliant sun. Ha, ha. I shout and raise my arm.

My face is black. Black, choked and swollen; nose and eyes disappearing into the skin, curling backwards over the edges of the mouth. Which is open. I am suffocating in my skin. My only breath coming out in a cry. Ha, ha. He is a weight on me. He is a burden. He calls me to play his tune and then deserts me. I am his puppet, hot and dancing under his manipulating fingers. No. No. I am black. Burnt black. 'Thou art to die.' So easy. The good die and we mourn. But who kills the evil; the poisonous, the dead men alive. Why should you live with your heavy poisonous hands? Pulling me. Dragging me. Tearing me down.

Others die. Why not you? You feel the black fingers on your throat. Face the black. Ha, ha. As I laugh. For I will laugh. I will laugh. I will laugh. Laugh. Laugh.

'April! April! Are you all right? April!' And she actually slapped my face. Only Jenny would do something so conventional. And be so successful. I became aware I was sitting on the edge of the bath laughing maniacally. 'Christ! You gave me a fright.' Jenny's face was thrusting at mine. 'Here, have a drink of water.'

'No, thanks.' I stood up and found my legs were shaking. Also my cheek hurt. The thought of the brutality in the slap upset me.

'Why don't you lie down?' said Jenny taking my arm. So I let her lead me upstairs. My head was vibrating as if the laughing hadn't stopped but merely retreated inwards.

'Can't I get you anything?' said Jenny. I lay on the bed and watched her drawing the curtains. I thought of turning her into comfort, talking for sympathy.

'No, thanks. I'm sorry I gave you a fright. I was tired.'

'Try and sleep.'

She went out. The room was dark. I didn't want to sleep. I wanted to think but the vibrations in my head were jarring my brain. I couldn't even remember. Besides, I felt incredibly tired. I couldn't have lifted a limb. Not even if the telephone had rung. I couldn't get up and go downstairs.

My pillow was so soft and the sheet which was rather worn and old folded round me like a silken sleeping-bag. I wished Jenny had left the curtains undrawn, so I could see the night sky. I felt curiously calm and relaxed. My exhaustion had turned into a great peace. The vibrations in my head had faded away leaving it empty and quiet.

I felt as I used to as a child at the end of a long summer's day in the country. All impatient energy drawn off and replaced by the sun and tired content.

Waves of self-satisfaction spread through my body.

I fell asleep.

29

SICILY

It ended. And I fell off the bed onto the cool tiled floor where I lay half-stunned, half asleep.

The sun was gentler when we woke. One of the blinds had been pushed open a little by a slight breeze. The sheets wound round the bed all the way to the floor where I had dragged them. A corner was caught round my ankle; it was still wet from my sweat. Tiredly I lifted my leg aside and then, using the bed as a support, swayed to my feet. My bones seemed to have pressed through my skin to the hard floor so that I was aching and bruised all over. My mouth was so crackling dry that I couldn't close it. I licked my lips and then dipping my finger in an un-drunk glass of *aqua minerale* ran it round my forehead and down my nose and chin. I was comforted by their familiarity. I thought I was in a country I didn't know, with a man I didn't know. I didn't know them but they frightened me. I stood swaying at the end of the bed with my eyes closed.

'Is that you, darling?' Lawrence mumbled and felt the sheet beside him like a Hollywood husband.

Probably not, I thought. It depends who you mean by 'darling' and you didn't say it reverentially like you do to me. It sounded more like a habit.

'To be continued in our next,' said Lawrence, sitting up suddenly so that I gave a jump and felt my eyes open wide. 'How sad it is after the event.' 'Like a tired piece of uncooked rhubarb,' I said and then was horrified at my vulgarity till I realized I hadn't spoken out loud. My bitterness took me by surprise and I sat on the bed apologetically. Mistaking it for affection, Lawrence drew me towards him.

'Now one hunger is satisfied, how about the next? Why don't you order me the most delicious bowl of pasta?'

'Can't we go out?'

'Like this?' He laughed. 'Haven't we filled our sight-seeing quota yet? Or are you planning a book on it?'

'It just seems a pity when there's all that experience waiting outside.' I was casual as if it didn't matter either way. But it did. The room was stifling me.

'Did I love you well? Are you glad you're with me?'

'Of course I am.' I turned to the telephone. 'What kind of pasta do you want?'

'Spaghetti like your hair.' He held onto a fistful and pulled it a little.

'Good strong stuff this; not overcooked at all.' He gave it a lick. 'And with a nice tomato sauce or perhaps, since we're near the sea, *alle vongole*. No. No. I've got a better idea.' He sat up enthusiastically. 'Order *gamberetti*. I haven't had real fresh *gamberetti* since I was last in Naples. Yes, that's it. *Spaghetti al burro* followed by *gamberetti*, followed by *frutta fresca*.' He lay back luxuriously.

I moved my head as gently as I could with the rage inside me. I gripped the receiver and with Lawrence beside me, now stroking my leg, now rolling on his back and sighing with pleasure at the ceiling, I gave out tight fierce little instructions. He laughed at my staccato spelling

135

out syllable by syllable, thinking it was to make myself understood. He didn't understand it was the clipped accent of self-control. When I had finished I went to the bathroom. It was closely tiled in dark green with fishes swimming round the rim above the bath. It was soothing and as my fingers fumbled for the taps, I realized there was no light. I had pictured the decor from its replica at the Palermo Jolly Hotel. It gave me an odd sensation.

'How's it in there?' shouted Lawrence lazily from the bed. I could imagine him negligently propping himself on his arm.

'Dark.'

'The fuse. I forgot.' He sounded amused. 'I'll order a candle.'

I found the taps and listened as the water poured out. I sat on the lavatory seat and watched it in the dark. I watched the noise. I had lost all will to move when the door opened and a candle appeared round the corner. The hand extending it was cuffed in white. It must be the waiter's. Hastily I wrapped a towel round me and took it.

'*Grazie.*'

'*Prego.*' The voice was startlingly near, then the out-side door closed.

'Why did you let the waiter bring me the candle? I didn't have any clothes on.' I went accusingly into the bedroom, glad really to have an excuse for contact.

But Lawrence was on the telephone.

'...surely you can get her back? She can't have got far ... at least till I'm with you.' He seemed involved and irritated and not at all vague like he was with me. Eventually he saw me and his expression changed to a slow questioning, but his eyes stayed remote. He pointed at the telephone and shrugged his shoulders.

I went back to the bathroom and got into the water which in such a hot climate was far too hot itself. I lay back and watched the candle reflect against itself in the mirror above the bath.

'My beautiful sea nymph,' said Lawrence coming up to the side of where I lay. 'I'm sorry about that. It was London. I thought it would take hours, but it came through just like that.'

'What's the problem there?' I asked, picking up the soap and letting it drop with a splash into the water.

'My wife.' His expression changed once more from romantic to involved. 'The au pair's run away with some man twice her age and left her in the lurch.'

I laughed, ironically.

'Just like us.'

'She'll come back, of course.' He either hadn't heard me or wouldn't hear me.

'Of course.'

'You look so comfortable in there, I think I'll join you.'

'I'm getting out,' I said. And rose so eagerly out of the water that a great wave swished over the end of the bath. I also bumped into Lawrence who held me close to him and murmured, 'Smooth, round body.'

'It is just like us. That au pair girl. You know it is.' I flung my wet hair backwards so that a strand cut across his nose.

'Don't insult yourself. Our au pair is fat, has long greasy hair and cries all the time.'

I went to the door. It was too much to admit how like myself that sounded. My cowardice made me more angry. When the door opened and the waiter came in for the third time, I shouted, 'Please knock!' He looked at me without reaction and put down the tray he was carrying on the end of the despoiled bed. Then he looked at me again and this time his eyes were direct and black. I realized as usual I was wrapped only in a towel. Oh, God! What did he want? Why did he stand there, looking like that? Then I saw he was jangling one hand in his pocket. Of course, a tip. Humiliated, I went hurriedly to my bag strewn across the dressing-table and rifled about for some change. I had none. I turned round again and opened my hands apologetically. He stared at me coolly with all the beauty of his small dark face and its fine thin mouth. How blousy I must seem to him! He turned suddenly as if he was bored with the whole idea of me and went out. I rushed after him and locked the door.

The tray, steaming fishily, sat on the end of the bed. I looked at it with disgust.

'Your food's here,' I shouted and then dragged a clean dress out of my suitcase. The case fell on the floor and a whole bunch of my ugly striped hair rollers fell out and rolled across the floor.

'What a succulent smell,' gloated Lawrence, coming into the room all nude and glorious. 'And they've cooked the *gamberetti* in their shells. Perfect!' Stepping over my sordid jumble he placed himself neatly in bed and held out his arms.

'The tray, please.' He smiled.

I handed it to him. In my unattractiveness unable to be anything but a slave. When I looked again I saw to my surprise he was wearing large horn-rimmed glasses. In one hand he held a fork neatly bound in spaghetti and in the other a copy of *La Stampa*.

He looked at me over the top of his glasses.

'You look a bit distraught,' he said. 'Aren't you eating?'

138

'No, well ... a little.' Mumbling, I got into the other bed as the place least likely to attract attention. I sat there in my underclothes and tried to be soothed.

'I love this paper. What invention!' He chuckled and read out loud: 'Princess Margaret is pregnant again—with twins.'

'Oh, yes.' What were we doing sitting in bed in a hotel in the middle of a dry arid plain? I could see through the window three men on the top of the new building with what appeared to be an enormous television aerial.

'Famous surgeon runs a brothel in Hong Kong,' revelled Lawrence. He pushed aside the empty plate of pasta and prepared to tackle the pink and scaly prawns. I looked with disgust as he pulled at their whiskers and hard pointed tails. He piled up the little sausages of soft pink flesh until he had enough for a good mouthful. Then chewing lustily he picked up the paper again with his un-fishy little fingers. His eyebrows flexed up and down, reflecting the movement of his jaws. He laid the paper down again and built a fresh pile of *gamberetti*. 'Any of that wine left?' he asked.

'I'll ring for some.' I picked up the telephone, delighted to be no longer watching him. Besides, if I couldn't persuade him to go out of the room, I would have to get drunk again. This time the voice at the other end of the line spoke in perfect English. I was flustered and couldn't remember whether *vino* was my language or his.

'White or red, madam?' he enquired patiently.

'Oh, either,' I said, tangling my fingers in the cord. At last I managed to get it back on the hook. To divert myself I chose a little two-inch pear from the fruit bowl and put it, core and all, into my mouth. Lawrence had finished eating. He wiped his fingers on the paper napkin. He

139

flung down the magazine but didn't bother to take off his glasses.

'Well, well! This is a holiday!'

'Don't you feel guilty?'

'Guilty? What about?'

'The au pair girl and your wife...'

'You're not still thinking of that dreary au pair? She was just a rather sordid foreign girl good for a night at most who trapped some poor old man into running away with her. And don't tell me that's like you. Us. Come here a moment.' He pulled me over to his bed, ignoring my reluctance, not noticing it, putting it down to shyness. He liked my shyness—like a wild creature, always surprised. 'Look at yourself,' he said, pointing my body to a mirror on the inside of the cupboard door.

'No,' I said. 'No, I hate looking at myself.' I twisted round awkwardly. I looked at myself obsessively, endlessly searching, trying to learn—when I was by myself. I knew my expression then; it was calm, profound, dignified. I knew what it would be like now. I squeezed my eyes tight shut. If I looked, I would see Lawrence behind me, with his arms held commandingly round my bare waist, with his hair which he had not combed since we made love, topping my own—ragged, still wet, abandoned. I didn't want to admit it; that I was there in his arms. So I squeezed my eyes shut and cried out again:

'No! Let me go! No, I won't!' I twisted and turned.

Lawrence thought I was joking. He laughed and held me tighter.

'Quite a little wild cat, aren't you? If you could see yourself now you would be surprised.'

Couldn't he understand! I snatched a great handful of

hair with one hand and clawed at his cheek with the other.

'Ouch! You're ruining my beauty. April! Stop it! What's the matter with you?'

At least he wasn't immune to pain. He let me go so suddenly that I fell forward onto the floor. I scrambled up quickly and stood with my back to the mirror. I pointed a finger at him which shook like a piston:

'Now you see. I won't look at myself. I won't.' My mouth and throat filled with water which forced itself up in small spouts through my nose and mouth. I was crying. I took back my shaking, pointing hand and rubbed it round my face like a child so that it was all wet and dirty with my tears.

Lawrence had taken off his glasses and was touching his cheek where I had scratched it as if he expected flowing blood.

'I told you,' I said, hiccoughing so hard that my stomach jumped. 'I warned you. Oh!' A wail was forming inside me. A lament I couldn't control. 'I'm sorry. I'm sorry. I didn't mean to hurt you.'

'Shut up!'

I stopped dead. Silent, immovable.

'Come here!'

I walked to the bed. He held out his arms to me. I climbed into them. 'Just shut up and lie still.' I lay in them with hardly a breath going through my body. Obediently, I lay in his arms. Perhaps I slept. 'There you are,' I heard him say, and it seemed much later. 'You were just worn out and drank too much wine without any food. Go and wash your face and I'll order something more to eat.'

I was obedient. I was obedient. The peace of it. The stillness and peace. The room was quite cool now and dim. But the lights had come on again in the bathroom. I cleaned my teeth and washed my face and brushed my hair. It hung obediently in smooth lines. I went back to my own bed; tidied the sheets. Turned to his bed and tidied that. He sat quietly inside it. Reading another news-paper with his glasses slipping a bit down his nose. He had draped a dressing-gown round his shoulders. Eventually he looked at me.

'Feeling better now? I don't like to be a schoolmaster to you of all people. The food should be here in a moment.'

'Yes,' I said, settling myself into bed with the two cushions placed evenly behind my back and the folded sheet pulled straight across my breasts. Perhaps if I stayed quite still I could preserve the peace.

30

ENGLAND

John hovered outside the teachers' room.

'April, that weekend you mentioned. I had an idea.' He looked deprecatingly round the teachers' room. But I noticed he was wearing a new pink shirt.

'What?'

'You see, actually our house is just about *en route* to you and I thought perhaps we could drive down and stop there on the way. We'd love to have you. My mother's longing to meet you.'

Obviously he had the whole expedition planned.

'I didn't know you had a car.'

'I just bought it. Second-hand. Off a friend who drove it all round Africa so it should be all right for Dorset.'

'Why not?' I said. And we arranged it.

In the classroom, my pupils had their desks pulled back for the play rehearsal I had promised them. As the end of term approached, they became more enthusiastic and secretive as if the sight of their near independence reminded them of their private personalities. But I didn't take the same obsessional interest in them I had before and sensing this they were no more noisy in their new-found confidence.

The girls hardly ever offered to carry my books for me now. All the children stood up silently when I came into the classroom.

'No rehearsal today, children. Let's put the desks back quietly.'

Only Leon, Leon with his shiny black features, his turned-up bottom, his insistent voice, gesturing hands, continued to plague me.

'But miss, when are we going to?'

'It's arithmetic, Leon, not acting.'

'But miss, we'll never be able to do it if we don't rehearse.' He became whining and reproachful. I had been ignoring his pleas for days. I knew he thought of nothing but *Othello*, I had watched him practising in the playground. I had also noticed Lauren, my Desdemona, become aware of how he watched her so that she was nervous and avoided him. 'Miss,' she said once, trying to slip her hand into mine, 'will you tell Leon to get off my back, please miss. It gets on my nerves, miss.' And when I told her not to be silly she had swept off in a huff with an over-the-shoulder Parthian shot: 'You're stuck up, miss. That's what we think you are, stuck up.'

And now Leon stood by my desk waiting for me to act like a fair-minded teacher and live up to my promise.

'You did say I was Othello, miss. And I've learnt all the words.'

He had never seen his shimmering turban. I had pulled it apart stitch by stitch. I had put the emerald brooch into the dustbin and hidden the feather among some paper flowers that stood in the fireplace.

Children are not given explanations. They are used to the irrational acts of adults. I didn't have to tell them why we would not do *Othello*. Nevertheless, I guiltily created an excuse.

'I'm afraid Mr Chitty doesn't like the idea of us doing *Othello*. You made so much noise when we tried to rehearse. He thinks *A Midsummer Night's Dream* would be more suitable.' My voice trailed off. I don't know why I thought they would care either way.

I looked across at the class. They had already re-lined the desks and were settling down with comics. I looked down for Leon. At first I couldn't see him and then I realized he was standing right beside me. It made me jump to see him so close and silent. Then he took hold of the wooden-backed blackboard cleaner lying on my desk. He held it in his right hand and stared at me intensely. I couldn't look away.

'What's the matter, Leon?' I stuttered feebly.

The blackboard cleaner hurtled towards me. Dust flew out in all directions.

'I hate you! I hate you! You're like everybody. You pretend! You don't care! You don't care!'

The hard wood caught the bridge of my nose. Blood poured down my face immediately as if all ready for just such an occasion. My eyes felt as if they were attached by a piece of string and someone had jerked it tight. I must have gulped or shrieked or something. Little damp children's hands clutched my arms.

'Oh, miss! Miss!' I heard all around me like cicadas on an Italian evening. I fell smoothly and quietly to the floor.

I felt as if I was being unwrapped from a black cocoon. Each layer was lifted gently apart and laid aside from my body. Gradually I became aware of light and then my arms began to swim.

'Rest now. Try not to move.' The thin veined webs slid from my eyes which opened into narrow visor-like slits. It gave me a rectangular view of the figures round me which were John first and Iris and Mrs Smith close behind. I gulped for air. My nose, part of the visor, was iron.

'That's right,' said Mrs Smith, 'deep breaths through your mouth. You'll be all right.'

'I don't think it's broken,' said John meditatively. And I noticed Iris stroking her own nose.

'It looks all right,' she agreed. 'Just swollen. That terrible little boy.'

'Oh, no. It was my fault.' I tried to sit up but a sledge hammer inside my head knocked me backwards again.

'No, now, none of that.' Mrs Smith put a roughened hand on my brow. 'John, don't you think you ought to take her home. I'll look after your class. April's can stay out in the playground till it's time to go home.'

John's car still had a sticker saying African Safari on it. The gear lever had a tuck at the top. He drove very slowly changing gears into traffic lights. I began to feel better. I looked forward to lying on the sofa in the flat with a cold compress and a reviving drink.

'Well, what was all that about?' Unfortunately I looked too well on the sofa. My eyes had opened again from small screen to Cinerama. John was life-size. He sat in my flat with one elbow on his knees which were rather apart and an enquiring expression on his face.

'It had all to do with something...' I said weakly. And paused. 'I think I could sleep now.'

'You know, you may get in a bit of trouble with the head.'

'Yes,' I murmured with an expression denoting acute pain.

'If your discipline had always been good...'

'I know...' my voice faded painfully. 'Sleep...'

John got up at last and stood looking down at me. I

closed my eyes. 'I'll see what I can do anyway.'

'Thank you.' I smiled totteringly and watched him leave the room. The door slammed downstairs. I stood up at once holding my head in my hands like a china cup. And walked stiffly to the telephone.

'Mr Mann's office.' The sprightly voice pierced me between the eyes.

'Could I speak to him, please?' I didn't need to muffle my tones. 'It's his niece,' I offered as an afterthought.

'Yes?' I hardly recognized Lawrence's dour tones. Clearly my 'niece' had signified nothing. 'Who is it?' He sounded even more impatient. I was about to put the receiver down. But my intense breathing must have carried through his office shell.

'April?'

'Yes.'

'Well, it's lucky you're not my wife.' He laughed.

'I've decided to leave school.'

'What? I can't hear very well.'

'I'm going to give up teaching.'

'I think I should ring you back. This line isn't very good.'

I was not going to be put off. I cried out through the buzzing in my head: 'When are we going to Sicily?'

'Yes, certainly. Perhaps we could meet sometime this weekend.' His voice was official, cold. Again that voice I didn't recognize.

I retaliated desperately: 'I'm going away this weekend,' hesitated a moment and then added on a rising shout, 'with a boy-friend!' But the telephone had clicked and I was left with my empty cry.

31

SICILY

Lawrence switched on the reading light. So I switched on mine. It had become black outside. I could hear the noise of the streets change from a rhythm of trucks and cars and workmen straddling the building to a softer jumble of cars and people occasionally exploding into a harsh roar as a motor bike or a parade of motor bikes went by. I still held my comb and I ran it through the end of my hair every now and again. We were four stories up, I remembered. Quite remote in our room.

Lawrence read quietly without any expression.

The food came. I believe it was brought by the same man who came before, but I didn't look up as he placed the tray on the end of my bed. Lawrence handed him 100 lire.

I ate the food slowly, mechanically, chewing each piece—I didn't notice what it was—ten or twenty times. Once I counted and I reached twenty-three.

'All right?' said Lawrence again, just looking up for a moment. 'It's wonderfully peaceful in here, isn't it?'

I pushed the tray back to the end of my bed and sat once more with my arms close to my sides listening to the sounds of the town outside and watching the dark patch of sky. There were no stars.

'Happy?'

I sensed he was smiling at me. But I couldn't see him

148

any more. I sensed his enormous flooding weight of content.

'Yes,' I said. And I was divided so far now from the voice inside me that had said before 'I want to go out,' had appealed, 'Can we go out?' had cried, 'I want to get out! I want to get out! I want to get out!' that I felt a smile across my face. Before I had laughed. I had laughed so hard in the bathroom in London that I had passed out. Now I merely smiled.

'Sleep well, my angel,' said Lawrence.

32

ENGLAND

Jenny was casual. She sat cross-legged on the floor with a pile of house agents' suggestions around her. Tom was very keen to find a house before they married. My voice reached her through a maisonette in Chelsea. 'Too small,' she told herself firmly and then looked up at me. I stood above her restlessly trying to convey the urgency of my request. I had failed totally.

'Not this weekend. It'd be no fun without Tom and anyway Pike's booked for the one after.' She sighed contentedly. 'I know we'll end up in Islington.'

I went to the telephone and dialled petulantly. John would be more malleable.

John was anxious: 'The point is, my mother sometimes works in the evenings. I'll have to check.' Then apologetic, 'Of course, the sooner the better as far as I'm concerned, you know that.' I could hear him smiling enthusiastically. 'But I do like to get arrangements right.'

I held the telephone a foot away from my ear to show myself how little I cared what he said. 'Well, I'm going to Dorset, anyway.' I was trying to hide my irritation under sweetness and only managing to kick over a pile of Jenny's papers.

'How's your nose?' said John. 'I'm sure this weekend will be all right, but I must check, that's all.'

'Fine. Fine,' I said. 'Let me know anyway. I'll be here.' I dropped the phone back.

'If you want to go away so much, this weekend...' began Jenny.

'Don't worry,' I said, looking at her new green boots. 'I love your boots. Would you call them pink or purple?'

'Green,' said Jenny unamused. So I went up to my bed. The telephone rang.

'April!' Jenny called. I ran down hitting my bare toe on a table at the bottom of the stairs. Without stopping to rub it I fell on the telephone. I wrapped the flex round my arm seductively.

'Hello,' I whispered.

'I rang straight through,' said John brightly, 'and luckily my mother was in and she said she would love to see us both. She's heard so much about you.'

'Oh, how very nice,' I said.

'That's good, isn't it? You sound rather far away. Are you all right?'

'My nose is hurting me,' I rubbed my toe. 'See you on Friday.'

'Oh, yes.'

I sat down on the sofa. Jenny caught three pieces of paper as they floated to the floor.

'I'm sorry your nose is hurting you,' she said.

I went up to bed again.

'How long your hair is!' John exclaimed on Friday.

'It's off duty,' I said. 'It expands.' I stood in the doorway to our flat and held out my case to him.

'You know you can be very difficult.' He opened the door to his car and I got in graciously. He put the case in the boot and I heard him try it twice to make sure it was properly closed.

'In what way difficult?' I said, crossing my legs negligently. We drove out through London, Notting Hill Gate and Olympia.

'Difficult as if you're afraid of me.'

'Afraid of you!' I heard my voice rise in shrill protest and felt ashamed. I looked at him apologetically.

'The lady doth protest too much, methinks,' he murmured smiling. I thought of the weekend ahead with foreboding. I had believed I could mould him to my tastes but already the steel rod was showing through the hempen coat. Even his unrestrained smile seemed a threat to my peace.

'It's the inside lane for us, I'm afraid,' he said contentedly as we reached the M4. 'The house is at Finchampstead.' I had never known anyone who took such a pride in facts. A voice inside me repeated to the sound of the wheels, 'So what? So what? So what? So what?'

I had always liked the M4, gateway to London Airport and almost anywhere. It was Friday evening and we were packaged into our lane by an impenetrable barrier of steel. It was hard to pretend I was leaving urban limits for the blue open spaces.

'Well,' said John, 'now we're on our way.'

We left the motorway in a sweeping curve and the sun was dropping downwards to the right. Neat hedges, green lawns in front of white houses, market gardens, pubs and garages—we had entered the no-man's-land of Bracknell, Ascot, Finchampstead. I had always wondered what it would be like to live with gnomes and television aerials for neighbours.

'Would you like a cup of tea?' said John.

'Well, actually I'd rather . . .' But to my surprise he was

152

already turning right towards a badly painted sign saying TEAS.

'But it's closed,' I suggested.

'Not to me,' he replied complacently and stopped the car opposite a door marked 'gulls', further down I saw 'buoys'.

'Come on,' said John getting out. The teashop was in a very small cottage with a conservatory added at the front. It stood just before a large roundabout. A succession of cars changed gears noisily as we stood at the door. A bell tinkled as John opened it. 'Tea!' he shouted jovially.

'Oh, there you are,' said a voice from inside. 'I left the door open so you could come right in.'

'I bet that's illegal with a "Closed" sign outside.'

I had been rather slow, I suppose, to grasp the situation. John's mother came to me with awkward warmth and grasped my hand.

'Well,' she said, 'this is nice of you. John gets so little gaiety.' I liked the idea of myself as a symbol of gaiety so we beamed at each other happily.

'Tea?' she said.

'One and six a pot,' I said picking up a menu.

'I could do with something stronger.' John strode through the conservatory to a smaller room behind.

'I did manage to get some sherry,' said his mother nervously, 'but I wasn't sure whether you'd like sweet or dry....'

It was sweet sherry and we sat there the two of us sipping it politely on either side of a pink lampshade while John went to get the suitcases.

'Have you always wanted to be a teacher?' she said.

'I hardly think of myself as a "teacher". I mean I'm not very good at it.'

'John's father was a teacher.'

'I see.'

'Fill up all round,' said John, chores over.

'You wouldn't mind just looking at the stove, would you, dear? It's been very odd today. Then I can get the supper going. I hope you like boiled beef, Miss . . . ?'

'April. And I love boiled beef.'

John and I sat on either side of the pink lampshade. There was a smart white telephone by his elbow. There was no chance of it ringing for me.

'Some friends are coming to supper,' said John. 'Incidentally, I expect you've gathered my father's dead. He had a stroke rather suddenly.'

I felt very sleepy. I hoped my eyelids weren't drooping too obviously.

'We've had a supply teacher while you've been away. A boy. I think he's homosexual, but since it's near the end of term he can't do much harm.'

'Are many of your friends homosexuals?' I asked lethargically. John looked intensely at the telephone.

'Not my friends . . . but I always thought my father had tendencies . . .'

'John!' his mother called from the kitchen. 'You couldn't get the big pan down for me, could you?' He jumped up at once. 'Mother finds things a bit difficult just at the moment,' he said.

So I went to have a bath. I would feel more able to cope with John's hidden depths after dinner.

His friends arrived very noisily as I was debating between trousers or dress. The noise decided me on trousers.

With darkness the conservatory had disappeared making the living-room seem even smaller than it had before.

154

Now it was filled with people. John jumped up: 'Was the water hot?' he asked with concern.

'Don't be indecent!' shouted a large man whose scarlet face topped a yellow shirt.

'To the pure all is pure,' remarked a lady, presumably his wife, with a long yellow face above a red shirt.

'Have you seen the garlic salt anywhere?' called John's mother from the kitchen.

'Aha! Real *haute cuisine*,' said the big man slapping his mouth. 'No scones and tea tonight.'

'Dick and Edie have their own place in Sunningdale,' John explained. 'I cook and Dick eats!' cried Edie.

I saw at once that I was eclipsed as a symbol of gaiety. I felt put out but decided not to sulk.

'What sort of people come to your restaurant?' I asked.

Edie immediately looked anxious as if she was sitting in front of a difficult exam paper and her big rather flat eyes stared at me blankly. Dick said, 'D'you mind if I help myself to another drink?'

'I mean, do you get stockbrokers?' I persevered and as no one answered, 'or golfers, perhaps?' Edie's face lightened; she pointed her glass at her husband:

'He's the golfer eating!' she cried triumphantly. 'He'll eat as many courses as he plays holes!'

'A man's got to survive,' returned Dick, proudly patting his stomach.

'On the table!' called Mrs Harvey from the kitchen, providing the signal for a charge of epic proportions.

'Tally ho!'

'How gorgeous!'

I was puzzled and followed more slowly. John took my arm: 'They don't like you to think they run their restaurant for money, you know, for customers. They are fun, though, aren't they? You mustn't let yourself be *overwhelmed.*'

The round table set in the kitchen—chintz at the windows, a candle on the draining board, a siamese kitten calendar and two similarly framed teacher's certificates— was so small that it was hard not to be *overwhelmed.* Early on, after the first course of potted shrimps, it became obvious that Edie and Dick had stopped in at the pub on the way. Eventually Edie admitted it, winning for herself a furious thump on the table from her husband:

'God, woman! Is our alcoholic intake so interesting that you're turning it public?'

Mrs Harvey grabbed at her bouncing glass nervously but in general seemed pleased at the liveliness of the evening. Every few minutes she looked at John and then sat back for a moment or offered some more food as if pleased with his expression. I thought he looked only slightly less uncomfortable than I felt. By apple crumble the room had become amazingly warm and our faces glistened colourfully. Suddenly Edie gave a shriek and pushed back the chair; she held out her wrist for all to see:

'Oh! no!' she cried. 'It's five past ten!'

'So it is!' Dick sprang up also. 'Where is it, John?'

John looked obstinate.

'I unplugged it,' he said.

'Unplugged it!'

'But we can't miss the ten o'clock!'

'It's easy to put back in,' said Mrs Harvey placatingly.

'Well ...' said John.

I found it a relief to sit quietly round a television set which was something I never did on my own. Besides, at the end of the news Dick and Edie rose firmly to their

156

feet. They were quite docile now as if world events had diminished their enthusiasm.

'Mrs Harvey, that was a delicious dinner. Thank you.'

Mrs Harvey turned off the television set. She looked at me as John saw off his guests. Mrs Harvey stared at me so I felt rather uncomfortable.

'Well!' she came to life busily and took up a handful of glasses. 'I'll be off to bed now. Would you like a cooked breakfast?'

'Oh, no.' Breakfast already. I lay back in my chair.

'Well ... I'll be off then.' I avoided another meaningful look. 'Night, all! Night, John!' she called.

John and I sat once again on either side of the pink lampshade.

'What has mother been saying to you?' said John.

'She asked me if I wanted a cooked breakfast.'

'Family problems are very boring to an outsider.'

'Oh, no.'

'My mother suspected my father's ... my father was particularly attracted to his pupils and she's afraid I may be too. She likes me having Dick because he's so masculine. She likes you too.'

'Because I'm so masculine.'

'Because you're so feminine.' John looked at his shoes gloomily. 'It must be obvious I'm madly in love with you.'

'Oh, no. That is ...'

'The trouble is, I think, my mother's right. I actually enjoy the look of little boys more than I do you. Little girls too, if it comes to that.'

'Well, if you like little girls too ...' I tried to be helpful. I wondered how he thought he was showing his mad love for me. Love, love, love. I waited for my heart to move or stop. Love.

157

'I could never touch you,' said John more gloomily. 'I simply could not put out my hand and touch your leg. You might as well be in a suit of chain mail.'

'How much have you drunk?' I asked meanly.

'You're quite right, of course. I've drunk far too much. Far more than I usually do. I don't hold it well either; it goes to my stomach. If you hear someone moving about in the night it'll be me being sick.' Lugubriously he put his hand to his head. 'My head aches already.'

I began to laugh. It surprised myself as much as him. He tried a weak smile.

'Sleep. Sleep. Sleep,' I cried and jumped out of my chair. All right then, life was a farce. Everyone miserable, everyone hiding their idiotic little perversities. John became an extension of Lawrence and me.

33

SICILY

I was still smiling when I woke up the next morning. I felt it lying across my face in an unaccustomed crease. I had been dreaming. The dream was still clear in my memory. Blue sky, blue sea and a row of golden pillars; between them I was walking—but not walking, rather floating, for my body was as light and airy as an angel's.

I neared the pillars and saw groups of people gathered there as if for some meeting to be held inside. Perhaps it was a church or a synagogue for they were dressed in long loose garments that reminded me of an illustration from the New Testament.

But they were waiting for me. I approached and some who were sitting on the steps stood up and looked towards me and the rest collected together in a welcoming party.

I waved my hand as I came to them and it felt like a flower in the wind. And then I recognized their faces above their loosely shifting robes.

My mother, my father, made up only of eyes warmly bending, eager with love and approval. They seemed at first interchangeable, sexless in their robes until I saw my mother, individual, wore blue shadow above her eyes.

I felt their kisses on my face. They kissed me first.

Then Jenny came. With Tom a shadow beside her and Pike a shadow behind him. But instead of black shadows they were white, pale reflections of Jenny's sun. For Jenny, as she kissed me, breathed scented sparks of light that caught and made a halo round our heads. She squeezed my hand.

And behind there was John. His robe, I noticed, hung a little awkwardly across his back. He pushed at it now and took me by the shoulders. He had grown taller so that his kisses on my forehead dropped from quite a height and tickled where they fell.

And their falling, like little bouncing drops of rain upon my skin, seemed to make their own accompaniment of tinkling sound. Until I saw the rows of smaller figures, lined along the steps as if for a photograph. Little figures clapping their hands cheerfully, pale pink palms coming together and then one of the smallest misaimed, beating air, and they all giggled sending a high ripple into the blue sky. I watched it float upwards like a piece of twisting smoke.

And when I looked down again, Anna, my sister, with her white marble forehead and cool black hair—except now it was transparent like glass against her cheeks—stood beside a pillar. Smiling at me. Smiling at me. Smiling at me . . .

I woke up in the reflection of that smile. I lay quietly guarding the reflection across my face. I lay still jealously guarding it.

But however silently I lay, it could not hold. I felt my mouth shrivelling, turning inwards, changing colour from palest pink to red. Becoming hard, attached to the rest of my body. For my body, try as I might, was returning too. Forcing itself up like pointed staves into my head till all the softness and light and airy weightlessness was gone.

'Slept well, darling?' said Lawrence from the next bed.

'All right.'

'Are you going to join me? Or nowadays does age come to youth?'

I sensed him turning on to his elbow although I couldn't see him—lying as I was, straight on my back. The day had begun.

'I'm coming.' I got out of bed and first opened the shutters. 'It's hot already.' I hung out of the window feeling the heavy air on my uncovered arms and neck. And then withdrew hurriedly as I saw a row of men forming up along a catwalk which hung along the outer edge of the new building opposite. They pushed each other dangerously for a better view. I half closed the shutter and got into Lawrence's bed.

'Well, what tourism have you got planned for us today?' He held me against his shoulder and his voice came out above my head. It was deep and loud. I lay there humbly. 'Twenty-five temples, sixteen churches, five mountain-top villages, seven museums, just to get us in the mood. Aren't I right, my dove?' He stroked my arm. 'I'm yours for the day—as long as it ends nice and early with a Jolly Hotel, a bath, a drink and a bed.'

And then as I said nothing: 'So,' he continued, heaving himself up, 'let's get the day in motion. The sooner it's begun, the sooner it's over. Breakfast, bath, a shave and a look at the map. How do you feel? Shall we sweat round this town, first? Then drive to Selinunte, exhaust ourselves at the temple—I believe there's a lido next to it where we could have a swim and lunch during the heat of the day; and make the Jolly Hotel in Agrigento by early evening. How does that strike you? It seems incredibly energetic to me.'

'You've planned it all out already,' I said. 'Can we buy a picnic lunch in the town here?'

161

'Greasy salami and old smelling cheese.' He groaned. 'I suppose it'll go down with enough wine.'

Lawrence went to the bathroom and I found the map in his suitcase. With it a small guidebook. 'Castelvetrano—this sleepy dusty town ... where the body of the bandit Giuliano was found in 1950 ... Giuliano has become a symbol of the individual's rights against tyranny of all sorts—governmental, civic or mafioso.' This sleepy, dusty town ... Breakfast came, brought this time by a young boy who looked at me nervously and was in and out as quickly as possible. I turned to 'Selinunte'.

'Temples A. B. C. D. E. F. G.' No romantic names. I shut the book and poured myself a cup of coffee.

34

ENGLAND

John felt so ill the following morning that he didn't trust himself to drive. Mrs Harvey seemed pleased by his condition and suggested roguishly that we should stop for a pick-me-up on the way.

'Thank you very much for having me,' I said.

'Well, it was quite gay,' she said between chopping parsley to fill the herb omelettes she made for her lunchtime guests. We spent some time discussing how to make eggs go further while John made himself ready to face us. I boiled ten eggs which she said would do for all her salads, however many called. I warmed to her in the strenuous practicalities of her day and quite regretted leaving.

John slumped in the car seat beside me. His car was very peculiar so I had little time for sympathy. It had a particularly irritating habit of sliding into the kerb. If it had been an animal I would have cursed and whipped it. Moreover, the seat tipped to the right so that I felt twisted in two places.

'I think you'd better stop,' said John, with sudden intensity.

I pulled up hurriedly. John disappeared into a straggly bunch of trees. He walked for a very long way and remained just as visible as he had been before.

'Don't mind me,' I shouted and leant against the other side of the car. A lorry roared towards me and when it came opposite hooted with a sort of grumbling obscenity. My good humour of last night returned. I put my hand through the car window and hooted back.

'I feel a little better now,' said John. 'I'll drive.'

I studied him. His sickly pale face made a nice contrast with his dark blue sweater. I thought he looked interesting and intelligent. He would take in anyone for a day or two, I thought.

'I don't think you realize just how honoured you are,' I said. 'You're the first man I've taken home.' Contact with the power of the wheel seemed to have helped him somewhat and he answered quite enthusiastically though still in a more languid manner than was usual:

'You're making me nervous.'

It was his languid manner, I decided, which made him seem more distant and therefore more intellectual and therefore more impressive. I hoped he wouldn't regain his customary health too quickly.

'How do you feel?'

'Just don't ask me.'

'Do you often drink a lot like this?'

'When I'm at home.'

'I know what you mean.' We were sympathetically silent for a moment.

'Do you remember what I said last night?'

'Do you want me to?'

'If you want me to.'

We passed through Salisbury before John could bring himself to speak again.

'The spire always makes me feel wonderful, unearthly,' I said, turning round in my seat as we left the town.

'I love you madly, darling April,' gasped John. I was still looking at the spire, its smooth sweeping height paling into the silky grey sky. I felt a lump in my throat.

'Thank you,' I said. 'I hope you enjoy your stay with us. I hope being in love won't spoil that.'

'Oh, no,' said John almost with his old fervour. 'As long as you don't mind.'

'Not at all,' I replied graciously as we passed by the great entrance to Wilton House. 'You know, of course, I have a married lover.'

But there is a sudden dangerously sharp bend in Wilton and John's mind was, in its imperfect state, trying to cope with that.

On reflection I was quite glad he hadn't heard and thought I'd save it up for later in the weekend. I wondered how shocked he'd be. The thought excited me.

A gentle west country rain was surrounding the green countryside as we reached home.

My father was practising his putting on the lawn, sheltered by a large multi-coloured umbrella. I was impressed myself by the picture he made. He certainly looked a real man. I wondered how many customers Mrs Harvey had entertained so far and thought that without her son beside me I would have found the whole of last night difficult to believe.

My father was waving his putter at us.

'Go on,' I encouraged John who seemed inclined to stop.

'Mother's making porridge,' my father said as we passed. But when we got inside the house—John held a suitcase in either hand—mother was talking on the hall telephone. She raised her eyebrows at us and waved her hand.

'I'll show you your room,' I told John who was silent and obedient. It struck me as shameful that my mother and I had been brought no nearer together by my sister's death. One might have expected that. But it seemed the reverse had happened.

John exclaimed at the view from his room. But I only saw father who had abandoned his umbrella which was stuck like a brilliant tree into the grass. He was lunging with his club as if it was a sword. John said he thought the hills to the left were definitely described in *The Return of the Native*.

Over lunch he developed the Hardy theme until I was quite proud of him. I wondered if I should be ashamed of my patronizing attitude. He bored my parents; although they knew enough to appreciate his knowledge if not to enjoy it.

I was only embarrassed by him once; he spoke into the silence which comes near the end of a meal:

'When I was a boy scout we came to Dorset for a week's camping but unfortunately I can't remember which area.' I pictured his bare knees with horror, and my mother said:

'Shall we have coffee in the drawing-room?'

However, my father put back the spoon into the Stilton and leant across the table:

'Are you still interested in the organization?' he enquired seriously.

'Not in the same way as I was as a boy,' John took a gulp of port which I thought brave if not foolhardy. 'But I do still help boys at school who want to join.'

My father, it turned out, was as often at Baden Powell House in Cromwell Road, London, as he was at his business (whose name I didn't know). So mother and I went to fetch the coffee. We sat over it in the drawing-room.

'Father said you were making porridge,' I began conversationally.

'He meant I was talking to Norridge, on the telephone, you know,' said my mother.

'Well, how is everything?'

'The washing-up machine has broken down,' said my mother vaguely.

Later John and I went for a walk. We headed up towards the hill he had admired.

'I had a most interesting discussion with your father,' he said with a slight flush of port still in his voice.

It was unfair of me to drape John's shoulders with all the qualities I expected in a man. However, being unaware of Lawrence's shadow like a giant vulture above his head, he walked with springy steps.

'Well, bitten by the snake seems to have worked,' he said.

I imagined the smokey smell of autumn fires and the air was silky cool. Every now and again a few drops of rain still clustering in the trees above us, sprinkled our faces. A slow-moving frieze of cows paraded along the top of the hill. We could still see my parents' house below us but it had become very far away. The lightness entered my head and made me gay for a moment. I ran a few steps—we were following a track through the fields—and then turned to welcome John. I stood with my hands clasped across my breast. The wind lifted my hair.

'I always seem to be running after you,' John said as if it was a joke. I bent down and picked a long dry grass to hide my annoyance. I had invited him with my abandoned steps to dally with me. I spoke with the grass between my teeth:

'Shall we camp up here tonight?' He didn't see the malice.

'I suppose you're in love with someone,' he said, flattening a piece of earth with his shoe.

I chewed on my grass and found that all the fun of revelations was destroyed. 'No,' I said looking directly at him. 'I don't know what people mean when they talk about love. I think the whole thing's wishful thinking.'

John became very gloomy at this and bit his little finger. We turned for home in silence. He was no doubt thinking of his problems and I was thinking of mine. I despised his as grey and small and ugly and floated on the back of mine as if they were a school of glistening porpoises.

I debated whether to ring Lawrence.

'Did you get wet?' asked my mother when we came back to the house. 'There was a real cloudburst here.'

'It didn't even rain on the hill,' John and I explained with the tenuous link of shared experience.

Should I ring Lawrence? Would it be a defeat to ring Lawrence? I went along to the bathroom. Most problems can be solved in the bath. Or in the warm afterglow.

Had Lawrence heard my defiant announcement that I was spending the weekend with a boyfriend? Even if he hadn't, my feverish tones would certainly disturb his comfortable weekend. Should I ring Lawrence? The evening became contracted to four words.

'Just a very small whisky,' I heard John's apologetic voice. We sat uncomfortably in the drawing-room.

It would be a pity to spoil that definite tactical advantage by ringing Lawrence quite so soon.

'It's so much nicer eating by candlelight,' said John. We moved to the dining-room.

Luckily I felt so drained of emotional energy that the temptation could not get its usual hold on me.

'Pass the salt to your father, dear,' said my mother.

168

Besides, Lawrence would almost certainly be out some-where on a Saturday evening.

'I see no reason why old customs should die out for lack of use,' said my father, lifting the port and brandy decanters from the sideboard.

'Oh, neither do I, sir!' said John rather tremulously.

My mother and I surveyed the broken washing-up machine. With one accord we abandoned it and made for the drawing-room.

And I discovered that, depending on how you looked at it, I either lacked the strength or had too much strength to ring Lawrence that evening. I sat down lethargically.

'Your friend seems very nice,' said my mother. 'I ex-pect he's an only child.' She sighed and stirred her coffee. Now, I was her only child. We both became very silent.

With no dramatic telephone conversation in view, the evening stretched ahead interminably. Interminably list-less conversations between the four of us.

Eventually, in despair, we accepted my mother's sugges-tion of bridge and some sort of shape was created between us. We discovered, for instance, that John had a strange talent for reading my mother's next move and even seemed to know which cards she held in her hand. This made them almost unbeatable when they played together. And I saw him, on the other hand, being taken aback by my total lack of competitive spirit and my happy-go-lucky way of playing my cards. And my father, the good effect of the boy-scout conversation having worn off, became irritated at John's method of chesting his cards which seemed to accuse his neighbour of trying to see them. By the end of the game, John, who was undoubtedly the best player, had made himself extremely unpopular with all of us.

'Very good, very good,' said my father grumpily. He handed John the score card. 'It seems we have a winner.'

'Past my bedtime,' said my mother wistfully as if feeling the lack of some honour due to her.

'Would you like a glass of milk?' I asked John.

'Oh, yes, if I may.' He was still excited by the game and his eyes shone. We went through to the kitchen and I bent down to the fridge.

'Oh, April!' John said, half clasping me as I stood up again. I chested the bottle of milk as he had his cards.

'Oh, April! You do need a protector!'

But his emotion was so strong that it carried him off without another word to his solitary bed. I drank the milk.

'Good morning, April! Good morning ...' said my father at the breakfast table, not bothering to hide the fact that he had forgotten John's name. Or perhaps following some planned policy linked to his defeat of the night before.

'Father cancelled the *Sunday Express*,' said my mother. 'I hope neither of you likes to read it.' She paused dramatically and poured out two cups of coffee. 'I am very fond of the *Sunday Express*.'

The papers, despite the absence of the *Express*, disguised the hours of Sunday more easily than the restless Saturday. However, by lunchtime they had all been piled up neatly on a chair for our cleaner to light the fires. My father, having been silent while he carved the roast beef —a task he very much enjoyed—piled up a small mountain of horse-radish sauce on the side of his plate and turned once more to John:

'Did you take part in the teachers' strike?' he asked.

'Our whole school closed down,' said John with pride.

'I see.' My father ended the subject heavily.

The climax of the weekend was produced by my mother when she discovered that the visitors' book was not in its normal position.

'James!' she called despairingly. 'It's gone! The book's been taken! April! Darling! What can we do?' She dropped telephone books on the parquet floor and joggled the telephone about so that it rang several times and the cook appeared nervously. I didn't see why she should be so keen to have John's signature when she had made so little effort to enjoy his company.

'Let him write it on a piece of paper,' I suggested eventually when it seemed she would disarrange the whole house and chain us forever before the front door.

'Thank you so much for having me, Mrs Leventon,' said John.

'April,' said my mother suddenly, taking my hands in both of hers, 'have you had enough to eat?'—it was three o'clock and we had done nothing all day but eat—'Let me get you an apple.' She ran to the dining-room; she pressed its cool weight into the palm of my hand. 'You know this is a very sad time for the family.'

We both got into the car and drove away. I looked at John. His cheeks were now quite rosy and his expression pleased and eager. Obviously, as far as he was concerned, the weekend had been a tremendous success. His ludicrous overtures to me had been merely a 'good beginning'— carried out with as much success as his low tenor of life led him to expect. I could rely on more to follow. Far from amusing me, the prospect filled me with depression.

Nothing would ever change; nothing would ever break through my crystal ball.

171

I wished, after all, I had rung Lawrence.

'It was an absolutely perfect weekend!' said John, placing my case like a fragile piece of china on the floor of my flat. 'See you at school tomorrow, then!'

I watched him go impassively but the need for decisive action boiled inside me. How dare he assume he would see me tomorrow! I suddenly remembered my bluffing remarks to Lawrence about leaving school. Now I saw it was the only possible course of action. I must not pretend to be a teacher any more. I would shatter John's boorish confidence. I ran to the head of the stairs and shouted exultantly after his retreating back:

'Yes, see you tomorrow!'

I walked back more quietly. The weekend hadn't been wasted, after all. I was victorious. I had cut myself off from Lawrence. I had cut myself off from John. I had cut myself off from those horrible clawing children. I would start a new fresh independent life. Like Jenny with a smile always. If Jenny could do it, so could I.

I poured myself a generous glass of sherry in celebration.

35

SICILY

As we came down the steps from the hotel, three boys
passing on scooters swerved in towards us and came to a
dramatic stop. With their feet planted on either side of
their bikes, they leant forward and watched us pass. I had
on a yellow dress spotted with scarlet strawberries. It was
a short dress so that I would be cool. They watched my
legs with silent concentration as I passed. I changed sides
with Lawrence so that I was shielded from them. But
as we walked down the main street of the town they followed behind us.

'Look!' I said to Lawrence.

'Take it as a compliment.' He held my arm cosily. 'I do.'

A row of trees ran down the broadest part of the
street. At the end there was a church. A humble church
in brownish stone with a little carving on the façade, and
two pillars set into the wall. I peered curiously into the
dark entrance. For parked beside it was a shiny black car
tied about with white ribbons and wax flowers. A great
bushy garland of leaves encircled the radiator.

I peered inside the church. And first there was the smell
—of incense rolling towards the light in waves; and then
there was the music—a deep rumbling organ, coming as if
from the floor; and then as my eyes grew accustomed to
the dark, I realized it wasn't dark at all. It was lit by tier
upon tier of candles which embraced the altar like a
gigantic wedding cake and continued down the aisle with
huge candlesticks wound in ribbons, white and silver,
tied with flowers. And above the aisle, hanging down to-

wards it like the pennants of a magnificent crusading army were swooping folds of velvet, scarlet, pale blue, white, pink, all edged in silver tassels that twitched and glittered in the candle-light.

'Oh, Lawrence!' I breathed. Glancing round for a moment. But he wasn't there.

And I turned back again quietly for now I could see the two figures in front of the altar. They knelt on either side of it. As still and perfect as the carved and painted images that stood in the niches above their heads. His suit was black—as black as her dress, laid round her in a perfect circle of lace, was white. On her head, small and neat above the ballooning white, sat a diadem of glass stars from which more lace, drifting from the stars like the milky way, flowed down her back.

Yet they must have been poor people. For now I looked at the crowds filling the dark pews. And except for one or two in the front who had an assorted collection of petals tied into their black hair, the women were dressed in the same sort of clothes as I had seen on the streets: heavily patterned overalls buttoning down the front with only a small piece of black lace securely gripped across their heads to show they were in church; and the men, there were very few of them, wore the usual shapeless black or brown suits; while the children, dark skinny limbs jutting out of turquoise and crimson dresses, ran unrestrained in and out of the aisle.

The congregation seemed another world from the figures in white and black posed so still where the glittering cascades of candles reached to the ground. Their full face was given to the priest whom I had not noticed before, so much was his pale brocade part of the ornamental altar. But now he separated himself and lifted above his embroidered sleeves the pale wafer of the host and the silver chalice of the blood. A bell rang twice. The organ no longer played. There was complete silence. And then, suddenly, with a jumble and an eager rush the congregation rose and standing with their arms folded broke into a great harsh wail of song. Tuneless, more like the cry of animals than of humans, it made its own heavy rhythm in an endless repetition of words. '*Agnello di Dio che togli i peccati del mondo ... Agnello di Dio che togli i peccati del mondo ... Agnello di Dio ...*'

Goose-pimples started along my skin and my throat burned so tightly that I put my hand to it.

'I thought I'd lost you.'

I didn't turn round immediately because the tears waiting in my head would have spilled quickly at the sight of him. Lawrence, standing, waiting.

So I turned first the other way, as if unsure which side he was, and so I saw the three boys sitting on their scooters watching me. They were fixed in their positions. They had been there all the time. I jerked round to Lawrence.

'I'm sorry.' I pushed him nervously to the doorway of the church. 'Just look how beautiful it is.' It was silent in the church again, except for a baby who had begun to cry somewhere at the back.

'I was right down the street before I noticed you had slipped the leash.' He seemed quite amused. After all, it had been only a few seconds that I had stood there, gazing, staring. 'A real Sicilian marriage indeed.' Lawrence glanced in and then drew me out along the pavement. 'The one day they let their women take the stage. They certainly make the most of it. Hocked up to the eyebrows, I should think. Poor things.'

36

ENGLAND

I kept to my resolution. I did not go back to school and I did not see Lawrence for a whole week. In fact, I saw nobody except Jenny occasionally.

School was easy—my resignation was accepted with a humiliating lack of argument. John rang, but that was easy too:

'Oh, no!' I fluted in absurd imitation of Jenny's aristocratic tones, 'April went away. She went away for a long, long holiday.' And at least John showed signs of regret not to say mystified dismay:

'Are you quite sure? I mean, I thought ...'

'Oh, yes. Quate, quate sure. I believe she wanted a total break.'

Lawrence was particularly easy to deal with because he didn't ring.

It was a strangely hot week for September, and I spent most of it lying on our roof watching the flakes of soot form a protective covering over my bared skin through which the sun had no hope of penetrating. My sweating body left a grimy imprint on my towel.

I was, however, looking ahead with optimism to the weekend at Jenny's home.

Jenny's family home was an hour's train journey from London. She always went by train because her mother, Lady Cole, had insisted on it when she was a debutante and prone to wild young men in yellow sports cars. And even though Tom drove a grey Vitesse with an eye on the shape of a speed limit, he still was not trusted.

Tom, Jenny and I were met by her mother at their local station on Saturday morning. The heat continued. The sun shone, the birds sang and she wore a straw boater trimmed with daisies.

'Darlings!' she cried, flinging open her arms. 'How glorious to have you all! Pike has already arrived and is sitting on the terrace in a deckchair with sunglasses and a newspaper, just as if he is watching cricket.'

Tom who was manfully wielding all our cases, put them down and gave her a kiss, having some difficulty with the brim of her hat and I wondered hopefully if I could get away with a handshake. I didn't, and was surprised by the youthful elasticity of her skin.

'Well,' she said, leading us to the car, 'how is everything? I couldn't wait to see you all so I had to meet you myself.'

The car—half loose-box, half-car—smelling richly of dogs and saddle soap, bounded forward as Lady Cole let out the clutch with amateur enthusiasm. Her fear of cars didn't extend to her own driving. But as we zigzagged along high-banked lanes, where the hedges tangled with glistening blackberries, I sat back happily. Tom and Jenny, I noticed, were holding hands and swaying in unison like two in a tango. It was exhilarating to be in someone else's countryside. Only competing with the changing greenery. Only answering to the name of Jenny's friend—with a hint of romantic interest towards Pike.

Pike, himself, shedding his cricketing calm, greeted us at the driveway entrance like his master's alsatian. Running beside the car and trying to grab Tom's hand through the window and finally as we hit the gravelled sweep in front of the house yelling to Lady Cole: 'Ever been go-kart racing? Together, I guarantee we'd slay the course!'

I saw why she liked him.

'Really, Pike,' she shouted back, putting her head out of the window and bringing the car to a jumpy stop, 'I'll call your bluff one of these days.'

And now a real alsatian appeared, followed closely, like the lackeys behind their master, by two terriers.

'Hello, Pike,' said Tom, putting down his load of cases once again and shaking hands formally. 'Good drive?'

I turned to Jenny:

'I *am* glad I came,' I said warmly.

'I knew you would be,' she replied smugly but a little diverted by Tom who was wrestling Pike for a suitcase he held goadingly above his head.

'Well, I'd better see how lunch is going,' said Lady Cole, gracefully side-stepping the boys. 'Jenny, April's in the pink room with rosebuds.'

I felt immensely tired standing there in front of the pretty stone house with the curving lawn and flower gardens fading away somewhere into a field below. As if all the tendons in my limbs which before had been pulled tight like elastic were suddenly relaxed, sagging to the ground.

At lunch it was the same. We drank cider and beer out of silver tankards and at one point my head nodded forward and hit my shirt-front.

'Who's for tennis?' cried Tom after coffee when I had slung myself like a hammock across a large armchair.

'You must, April!' Jenny jumped on my weak murmurs of a rest. 'We need you for a four and besides, it's good for you.'

At first my arm bent under the weight of the tennis racket which scooped at the ball as if it was a spoon. I looked at the strings reproachfully but they were blamelessly taut.

'Brace up!' shouted Pike at my service which was the only stroke he couldn't take for me. 'I'll get my own back at poker this evening!' he added to Tom who was complacent in his four-games-to-one lead.

But after a while there was a rhythm to my play and the hardness of the racket began to extend along my arm. The sky which was blue with a dash of white where some clouds were gathering for dusk seemed to lift the habitual weight from my shoulders so that I began to feel I was swinging, light-bodied, in space.

'Watch, Popeye!' I cried, giving a great sabre-swing at the ball. 'And get this!' It roared viciously across the net, bouncing in and out of the tramlines with satisfying, unstoppable meanness. 'Bravo!' I yelled to myself, and Pike chorused:

'Keep up the good work, partner,' so that the afternoon took on quite a different turn.

'You realize I was Captain of Games!' I informed Pike boorishly as we won the final deciding set. Which, as a matter of fact, was perfectly true—just not the sort of fact that comes out in London.

'Were you really?' said Pike with admiration. 'You ought to play more, keep in training.'

We sat on the terrace eating fruit cake and drinking tea. The clouds had finally overtaken the sun, but it was still warm enough to kick off our hot gym shoes and gulp at the ice cream which followed the cake.

Tom and Jenny pushed themselves back and forward on a flowery swing seat. He had his arm round her and was amusing them both by tickling her neck with a silver teaspoon.

Pike, who had stripped to shorts, left his deckchair and flung himself on the grass in front of me. His strong-muscled chest was deeply sunburnt. His dark red cheeks with the heavy black shadows, which had seemed so unattractive in London, now in the countryside gave him the wild look of a gipsy. His thick hair had curled up in damp black ringlets on his forehead.

I laid back my head against my chair. The sky above the clouds was filling with streaks of mauve and pink and purple, which vaguely reminded me of something though I was too lazy to think what.

'Whoever wants to go inside?' said Pike.

'Why don't you just live here?' I sighed to Jenny.

'With Mummy?' she answered practically. 'Absence makes the heart grow fonder.'

The sky became a dark violet with only the smallest rim of scarlet still showing above the bank of clouds.

We wandered inside, up the oak staircase which creaked sympathetically with our aching legs.

'God,' I said to Jenny as I ran a bath, 'I haven't ever for years and years felt so absolutely *good*!'

'I must say you look about fifteen.'

I did. The mirror sparkled with my teeth and my eyes and my sun-flushed cheeks. Even my hair seemed to be celebrating in bouncing corkscrew curls.

'If you want to be really good,' Jenny slammed the bathroom door and then opened it again, 'you can give Mummy the pleasure of leading you to church tomorrow. It's a sweet little church. As a matter of fact, we'll probably be married in it.'

*   *   *

I wore Lady Cole's straw hat with daisies to church. She insisted, because it went so well with my white dress and white tights. She said it made her feel as if she had a young daughter again. Jenny and Tom walked behind, playing at Uncle and Auntie. Pike had overslept. He and Tom played cards till three a.m. I had been asleep then, already folded into talcum powder dreams, for three hours. I had woken early and wandered round the garden, feeling as if I was still dreaming. The dew lay on the lawn in misty cobwebs; a sprinkling of daisies clutched into tight balls waiting for the sun; the birds sang in fluted trills—unthickened by the day's dust.

Our little procession moved gaily down the driveway. The church was only a few yards from the entrance to the house. Jenny picked a yellow rose for Tom's buttonhole.

I thought of yesterday through a golden veil of sun. I considered plans for an idyllic life in the country. I thought of Pike with affection. I suspected I had risen in his eyes to the level of a 'jolly good sport'—after all I had even given up teaching. Or perhaps he had raised me even higher. His big hard hand had taken mine just before I went to bed and given it a very meaningful squeeze. I smiled at myself.

The church was very small with a square tower and a weather cock perched on the top. The stone was yellow and the remains of a Norman arch curved above the heavy studded door. Inside it was dark and smelled of must and candle grease and old damp stones. I could just see a few people in the small upright pews grouped towards the altar. The altar was brilliant with marigolds which crowded against the candles in golden bunches and made the yellow stone seem pale. We started forward.

Then the sun which was jumping in and out of the clouds came shooting, suddenly, through the narrow ruby windows on the left side of the aisle. A face, glowing red, turned round and looked to where we had let the door bang shut.

'Lawrence!' I said quite loudly and then coughed to hide it. But our feet were clattering on the stone-flagging and no one had heard or noticed.

We sat two rows behind him. His wife, uncovered pale hair, navy blue linen coat, handbag and gloves, sat beside him.

'I'm afraid I feel sick,' I whispered to Lady Cole and crept out of the pew. 'Don't. No, don't,' I said to Jenny who wanted to follow me.

I walked very, very slowly back to the house. I could hardly lift my legs and yet my head was hot and buzzing. I passed right by Pike who was swinging a golf club on the lawn, without being able to speak. 'My sisters always feel sick in church,' I heard him say sympathetically; so I must have looked ill. I went to the drinks standing on a table in the drawing-room and poured myself a large sherry.

'Just the thing before lunch, eh?' said a voice from a sofa. I had forgotten about Lord Cole who had hardly been seen over the weekend. But I didn't even have the energy to be embarrassed.

I went out to the terrace and sat on the swing seat. After a while, a bell started to ring, and sometime after that voices processed up between the rhododendrons bordering the drive and disappeared in through the front of the house.

Of course I now remembered what I'd pretended to forget before—tripping romantically through the dew, spat-

182

tering my eyes with the early morning sun—Jenny had found her job because Lawrence knew her mother, he had a cottage somewhere near.

I inspected my face in the base of my glass, now empty, and found the contents had galvanized my empty body into action. Tipping the hat with the daisies further back over my innocent forehead, I stepped through the french windows into the house.

'Oh, there you are, dear! Feeling more settled?' The drawing-room was streaming with sunlight and after-church goodwill.

Lady Cole got up from the sofa and took my arm: 'You've more of a colour now. Let me introduce you . . .'

Lawrence—I encouraged the thought—looked faintly absurd, in his roll-necked sweater and brown punch-hole brogues.

'Hello again!' he said, half-rising, half-looking. Though I knew by his hunched shoulders and jumpy feet that he was licking up the delicious embarrassment.

'And do you know Mrs Mann?' said Lady Cole.

She had thick legs, I noticed with relief. In well-bred stockings, shoes, but definitely thick. I thought of myself all in white and offered her a wispy smile.

'Lawrence likes your church so much . . .' she said, continuing the conversation.

'And dislikes your vicar's hour-long sermons,' said Lawrence from behind a large coloured handkerchief he had pulled out. I hardly needed to look out of the corner of my eyes to know what he was doing.

'How about a game of tennis?' Pike was bored. He sat with his legs apart tapping his knees.

'How far do you live from here?' I asked Mrs Mann. I was still standing in front of her. She had fair skin

183

wrinkling at the edges and all the edges turned down. Her pale hair would slowly become grey and only she would notice the difference. She looked sad.

'Go on then,' Lady Cole shooed at Pike. 'The young to the court and the old to the drink.'

Mrs Mann was answering me. She had a soft voice with almost a stutter:

'It's just a small cottage we have—no telephone. An escape from London for our daughter really. You know.' Her wrinkles turned up for a moment and disappeared. She seemed younger. I stared at her elegantly shod thick legs and wondered if she looked unhappy because of them or for some other reason.

'You ought to come down more often, Larry,' Lady Cole said. 'You'll get lazy sitting round London all the time.'

'Julia's the country-lover.'

So this is where she was when I went to their house, sat at her dressing-table. This was her green retreat, her countryside. I stared through the french windows to the Wellingtonia on the lawn. Its boughs sank mournfully in dark swaying folds.

'Come on, April!' Pike took my arm. I hesitated between images.

'My family has a house in Dorset,' I said.

I stood between Lawrence and his wife.

'How lovely for you! Dorset is so beautiful,' she smiled up at me.

'Come on! We'll really smash them today.' Gracefully, head bowed so that I only saw her legs and his shoes, I let Pike lead me away. 'Goodbye, sir, Mrs ... er,' he called over his shoulder.

Becoming more conscious as we left the room, I won-

dered if he seemed as uncouth to them as he did to me.
Or did he just seem young?

It was hotter than the day before on the tennis court.
My face and neck started to burn.

'Run!' shrieked Pike.

'Ha! Ha!' gloated Tom as I missed his service.

'It must be lunchtime,' I retaliated weakly.

They didn't even come down to watch us—come for a
stroll through the garden and watch the children playing
games. The blackness spread up from the tarmac surface
of the tennis court and threatened to engulf me. I had
changed into a pleated skirt and my knees, like fat pink
slugs, moved slower and slower under it. At last a bell
rang in the house.

'Hooray! Lunch! I'm famished!' Jenny boisterously
threw her racket into the air.

The grown-ups were coming out of the house as we
approached it across the lawn. Mrs Mann was saying: 'I
only wish we could, but you know what children are like
if you don't keep your promises.'

I stayed outside pinching snapdragons till they had
gone. When I got bored with watching the powdered
stamen spew out of the petals, I stared down at my gym-
shoes which had an unattractive sweat mark. I didn't see
Lawrence till his shadow crossed mine and his hand was
outstretched towards me. I raised my eyes unwillingly and
saw his wife was already in the car. I felt sick.

'I have the tickets,' he said. 'It will be for five days.'

'We haven't met for a week.'

'My darling! We leave on the 25th.'

'Did you come here to tell me that?'

'I came because you looked so virginal in church that I
wanted to rape you all over again.' And he grasped my

hand as if to shake goodbye, and my body became very hot.

'I'll telephone.'

I peered at him through the strings of my tennis racket as he walked away.

'Lunch-time!' called Jenny from the house.

I threw England behind me as easily as a tennis ball. I couldn't even hear its voices.

37

SICILY

We walked along the narrow pavement; side by side in the sun. I suddenly noticed how tall we were. Like clumsy trolls we towered above the cars that crawled along the street; while the people who passed us—stepping off the pavement to get a better look at the foreigners—could have used Lawrence's long legs as a bridge over their heads. I thought, now, how the bride and bridegroom in the church had been like dolls, china figures, from a mantelpiece. Lawrence could have placed them on his mantelpiece, holding carefully one in either hand. Kneeling on the palm of his hand.

'How about this shop for your picnic?' He separated a narrow curtain of coloured plastic thongs covering an entrance, and I went obediently through. Inside there was a small counter piled all around with cardboard packets and tins and bottles. A young girl was serving an old woman shrouded in black. They stopped talking and stared silently at us. The girl had a pale olive face with big ears from which hung little golden pendants. Above her plain wide mouth there was a firm line of black hairs. On her left hand which was laid flat and straight upon the counter she wore a wedding ring.

She smiled sweetly.

'*Buon giorno!*'

'Your glittering bride in a month or two.' Lawrence

spoke with such ironic emphasis that I was afraid the girl would understand.

But she dug enthusiastically among the boxes and tins for a stick of salami and chopping it carefully into little chunks watched me brightly for when she should stop. And she was so proud of a dried yet sweating lump of cheese produced from under the counter that I took that too.

'Bread and wine for me. Bread and wine,' said Lawrence mockingly as we went back to find the car.

The car was even smaller than I remembered and the sun had managed to creep round the edge of the Jolly Hotel so that the smell of hot plastic was overwhelming. I quickly rolled down the window.

'I see you're the sort who believes in letting in the heat,' Lawrence said.

'I was letting it out. We had them open yesterday.'

'Of course, my darling.' He squeezed my knee. 'I was only joking.'

We drove through the town and I didn't bother to point out we were being followed by the three boys on their scooters and that now two Fiats had joined them and a three-wheeled cart.

Lawrence had stopped talking again, disappearing into the duty of driving. Growing beside me in silence and size.

Only once he exclaimed: 'Blast!' as one of the scooters nearly forced him into a one-way street. Our street was also one-way leading out directly to the countryside and the sea. Our escort split up—some going ahead, some falling behind. I looked out of the window. How dry and yellow everything was! Even the plants seemed by nature yellow. A giant yellow cow-parsley choked up through the dust which, as we got nearer to the coast, became the golden white of pure sand. Then for a moment there was a flash of scarlet; just a moment and it was gone. A scarlet poppy left over from the spring. I watched carefully and a little later there was another. It reminded me of something. I looked down abstractedly and saw my dress, yellow with its brilliant spots of scarlet strawberries. I was part of it. Part of this yellow land with splashes of bloody red. I stopped looking out of the window and closed my eyes.

'Five kilometres,' said Lawrence. 'What time is it, my sweet?'

'Where's your watch?'

'In my right-hand pocket.'

He sat, hunched up in his seat, too big for his seat, looking straight ahead, as impassive and demanding as a buddha. He wore pale trousers that wrinkled tightly across his thighs and hips. I looked at the opening to the pocket. I would have to flatten my hand like a knife to get it in. His warm flesh would close round it like a wound. I put out my fingers tentatively. But they made a spoon. No knife.

'Here.' Lawrence lifted himself up from the seat. The back of his shirt was wet. I dug into his thigh with my spoon. I thought about flesh. How soft it is. Yet how tightly packed with sinews, guts and blood. How closely now it pressed against me. I dug with my spoon, but there was nothing there.

'It must be in the other one,' said Lawrence, easing himself back in the seat again. 'It doesn't matter. We must be nearly there now.'

'Lido di Marinello,' I read out. We had turned along the sea front into a string of pale-washed houses and shops. It was a small place. The street, obviously the only street, was narrow and sandy, the buildings low and square with two windows up, two windows down, and every space filled with little cars and scooters. I thought I recognized the boys from Castelvetrano, but they all seemed so alike with their bright coloured shirts, dark faces and neat slim bodies that I couldn't be sure. The house on our left blocked our view of the sea but every now and again there would be a roughly painted sign saying: 'Bagno Belvedere' or 'Bagno Azzuro' with some rails descending down narrow steps—almost ladders. I realized we were on a cliff above the sea.

'What a strange place.'

Although there was nothing unusual about the *Gelati Motta* signs, the little pink and blue houses, the lounging youths, I felt an uneasy atmosphere closing round, as if this small seedy resort was looking forward to something else. It seemed both dead and yet curiously vibrant. Perhaps it was only the odd contrast of the feeling of poverty which hung over everything with the brilliant youths and their shiny cars; the piles of rubbish collecting in front of the houses; the absence of lights or flags or television aerials or shopwindows piled high and overflowing outside with rubber balls, spades, buckets—or any other of the cheerful paraphernalia usually found in seaside resorts. Or perhaps it was the absolute lack of any growing things: no grass, trees, flowers, creepers; only the dried-out, washed-out colours. Except, that is, for the *gelati* signs.

There was one now on our right. And opposite it, overlooking the sea, a small square of tables covered by a half-complete ceiling of rush matting. No one sat there.

'We might as well stop here,' said Lawrence. 'Or we'll be out the other side.' He parked the car among the other cars and a group of boys—silent, no transistors, I noticed with surprise—watched attentively as I brought out our brown paper bags, sweating a bit with the cheese and salami.

It was twelve o'clock. Noon. And everything was very still. I followed Lawrence across the road and as he passed through the tables. They were made of thin wooden slats with curling pieces of worn lino tacked to their tops. A few chairs were scattered listlessly round; others were stacked carelessly in a corner. Lawrence leant over a rail at the far end. I pushed aside a broken chair and stood beside him.

A long way below us was a wide sweep of sand. We were on a much higher cliff than I had expected.

'I don't like this place,' I said with sudden fierceness.

'Not very inspiring, is it?' He didn't bother to turn round.

'I hate it.'

'Don't you want to go down to the beach?'

'Not here.'

'All right. Perhaps we'll find something better at the temples. Do you see them on the promontory?'

I glanced without seeing. 'Yes. Let's go there.'

A small man in a white shirt and black trousers was coming across to us.

'We might as well cool ourselves down with a drink now we're here.' Lawrence sat down at a table.

'*Prego*,' said the waiter.

The group of youths crossed the road and walked slowly past us. They stood with their backs to the sea watching us. Lawrence gulped back a Coca-Cola and then sipped a Punt è Mes. He wiped his face with his handkerchief.

'Well, are you going to read me some tourist details?'

191

'The book's in the car.' There was a smell about the place—of rotting food and bad drainage. Even the salt air could not kill it.

'These chairs don't exactly encourage one to stay.' Lawrence heaved himself up and the chair, as if his weight had been the last straw, tipped over behind him and collapsed into a pile of sticks.

As we walked away I heard the boys poking at it and laughing. Hurriedly I bent into the car and didn't look back. Immediately after Marinello the road divided and became smooth black tarmac; shrubs appeared on either side in cultivated precision and clean official-looking signs pointed to Selinunte ahead. The air was fresh.

'I really did hate that place,' I said again, now we had left it, a little surprised at the depth of my reaction.

'You've grown so vehement since we came to Sicily,' Lawrence laughed. 'I'd never recognize you for the gentle creature I knew in England.'

The black road led smoothly up to a sentry box caught between high wire fences. Behind us and to our left the bay curved round and down to Marinello. From this distance it looked like a charming postcard—picturesque and inviting.

A uniformed machine-like guard came out of the sentry box and gave us tickets. The road climbed up again and then we were in amongst the fallen pillars, great slabs of pale broken stone, heaps of carved corners, flourishes and whirls. Lawrence parked the car under a straw awning. There were only one or two other cars.

I found out why when we got out of the car. The heat was terrific, all-enveloping. It clasped round my head like a tight helmet. I brought out the paper parcels again.

'Oh, leave them here for the moment,' said Lawrence.

I looked at him over the top of the car. His face was crudely mottled and red and sweat from his forehead ran down his temples and into his side-burns. I looked away from him. We were parked, I realized, on the edge of the cliff, although a thick hedge of greyish cacti hid the sea from view.

'Come on,' said Lawrence, as I stood mesmerically peering at the fat and prickly leaves, wondering about the drop below, the ice-cold green sea. 'There're at least five temples to be got through here.'

The first stood, the only thing standing, for the rest of the ground was littered with fallen stone, about a hundred yards away. I started out towards it, walking fast, pretending the heat wasn't muffling my limbs like hot cotton wool, pretending to a youthful enthusiasm; pretending I was walking so fast because I enjoyed it not because I wanted to run. I wanted to run. I wanted to run away from Lawrence. I walked very fast.

I stood under the gigantic pillars by myself for a moment and felt their great weight as a strength behind me. If only he would never come again. I watched him come. What I hated most was the absolute knowledge I had of him. His height, the way his fine head, rather large Roman head, sat on his shoulders. His shoulders which sometimes seemed slumped, sometimes hunched, but never drew a direct line. Now they were hunched. His torso, fixed heavily on his hips as if still surprised to be so big. His legs, his legs I knew best; so very long and straight and strong, yet so ready to fold up, cross over each other, abdicate the burden of his body to a chair or better still a sofa or best of all a bed. He must have known about his legs or why else the pale tight-cut trousers? He was too old for tight-cut trousers.

193

Then his feet, now in old espadrilles, oddly small for his height. Small and workmanlike—more like hands really, with an endearing unmanly habit of turning inwards.

Except it didn't endear him to me. I watched him now come closer, place each foot carefully between the rubble.

Now his face was sharply defined. His eyes were direct, driving like a knife into mine. And yet I knew they only saw what his imagination drew for him. Sightless eyes turned inwards on his own romantic vision. Then why did I feel pierced? Could I not turn the dagger round?

'My Goddess,' he said reaching me. At last. How long had he taken? Had I run to the temple to wait for him so long? Or was it just a second?

'My Goddess!' He was very serious. He took my chin. I was still, my face rigid, my expression blank. 'Standing unapproachable at the temple doors.'

Yes. I was unapproachable. I couldn't stand with him. I walked briskly—a few paces to the next pillar as if to look at it. A flitting remembrance of my dream drew a picture in my mind, and then was gone.

'I do long for a swim,' I said over my shoulder. My voice was shrill. I stood facing the pillar.

'Well, you didn't like the lido.'

'It's so hot!'

'It's one-thirty ...'

I started walking to the end of the temple.

'We could swim somewhere else. I mean there'll be a beach the other side of the promontory. We could get down. Couldn't we? Couldn't we?' I sounded hysterical. I swung round for a moment. Lawrence was resting on a slab of stone. His legs were stretched out before him, crossed at the ankle.

'We could, I suppose.'

194

'Come on!' I cried. Trying to entice him. 'Look, here's a way down, I'm sure. We'll be all on our own.' I waited restlessly ten yards from him. 'Think of the ice-cold water.'

He got up. Because it was more effort to subdue me than his unwilling flesh.

We started along the path—once a Greek thorough-fare. The foundations remained: cobble stones, kerb stones, but now choked with dry yellow grasses or dark prickly bushes. I kept a few yards ahead. I could no longer bear him anywhere near me.

'Slave-driver,' he said once but feebly as if he had delivered himself into my hands.

I laughed without looking round and moved faster and faster.

38

Then I heard him shout, this time with enthusiasm: 'Some wine! I'll get some wine!' The tone of his voice stopped me. I sat down where I had been running—in the straggly bushes and sandy soil. He was coming to my command. And now he was running for the wine and soon he would run after me. And then with me? I sat down, breathless with power and exhaustion. A lizard rested on a stone beside me. His eyes blinked rapidly and his little stomach panted in and out. He was resting too; his eyes like mine glittered with excitement.

'I'm on my way!' The lizard jerked in a quick spasm of terror and was gone. Lawrence appeared at the top of the slope waving a bottle. 'Success!' he shouted.

'Hooray!' I cried, jumping up at once. How odd and unusual to be in the same mood as him. But I didn't quite wait for him to come up with me. I walked quickly until the Greek road lost its outline and a tangled row of wire cut across the bushes before me. Beyond it lay the sand and the sea. It was the other side of the promontory. The sand had no footprints across it. I wondered about the wire; it was strong and new-looking, four strands high. I wondered if the beach was dangerous and how we would get over it. Then I realized it was to keep trespassers out of the excavations not out of the beach. I climbed down and prepared to wriggle under it. With my ear to the ground I could hear Lawrence's heavy steps. He arrived above me, huge against the bright sky.

'I'll throw you over,' he said. 'Isn't this daring?'

'You try!' I cried laughing at his old-fashioned 'daring'; knowing how he would humiliate himself: 'You'll never do it.'

'And then the wine after.' He scooped me up and threw me over the wire like a cartwheel, leg after leg, arm after arm. I sprawled in the thick waves of sand; and the bottle came flying after. He stood the other side looking a bit dazed.

'And now how will you get over?' I shrieked suddenly, kneeling up and shaking the sand out of my hair. 'I've got the wine too!' I picked up the bottle and offered it reverently to the sky.

'Monster! Idolator!' he cried, recovering himself, and put a square espadrille on the bottom wire. It sagged almost to the ground. I leapt to my feet and started to run with the bottle. The beach curved round to the left and there were rocks lying jaggedly around; I didn't want the calm sea yet.

I sat on a rock with the bottle.

Lawrence came. Walking steadily. Sweating.

'I had to trample the wire rather,' he said. 'It is hot! Here, let me knock the top of that bottle off.'

I handed it to him without moving my body. It had become part of the rock, yet quivering, tense.

Lawrence shattered the top of the bottle. His strength on such an insignificant object was ridiculous. 'It's dangerous,' he said, eyes glittering. The broken pieces of green glass were brilliant as water among the pale dust of the sand. He tipped the gaping, shattered bottle to his throat and the red wine came spouting out. 'It really is far too dangerous,' he said. I watched as his throat which had been stretching up to accept the liquid, compressed

197

back into place and hid again under his face. I took up the bottle. The red stream gushed out, but instead of running neatly into my body, it caught on my nose and lips and chin spreading round the lower part of my face till it dripped off into the sand. I put my hands up and they too became smeared with wine. The sweet rich smell inflated my nostrils; my fingers rubbed together stickily.

'I'll swim now,' I said, pulling off my dress which was also wet. Lawrence spluttered at the bottle. He put it down in the sand and built a little wall round it. But I was already running to the sea.

The water flowed over me and ran off my body as the wine had done. Lawrence didn't like sea water; he hated anything that changed the temperature; that lowered the temperature. I put up my head and saw him standing on the shore line. He saw my turtle hump and paddled up to his ankles. He hadn't taken his trousers off.

Impermeable. Impervious. Again I was angry. I turned my back on him. 'Come here!' he called at once. And I could imagine him waiting lazily on the shore. Tipping the bottle, smiling in the heat. Content. Absolutely content.

I swam back and stood up in the shallow part of the water. But too far out for him. The salt sea had fixed my anger. I stood confidently letting the water drip down my legs and arms.

'Come in!' he cried. He sat on a rock waiting for me.

Haughtily, kicking sand in sudden spouts, I went towards him. 'Some wine, please,' I demanded standing a yard in front of him.

'You look magnificent,' he said, handing me the bottle. I knew I did. I did.

I drank the wine while the sun dried and tightened my

198

skin. I felt the moment hanging still.

'The inner man,' said Lawrence. 'The inner man! I wouldn't even refuse that salami now.'

'All right,' I hissed. 'All right,' I hissed again. Furiously. 'Let's go back. If that's what you want.'

Still obedient, but only just.

A narrow path curved round the promontory, at first threading the rocks along the shore-line and then gradually edging upwards. I thrust my dress back over my head and started up. Lawrence admired my bravado. I felt him like an audience at an opera, sitting back and admiring, confident in the flower he would throw at the end. Involved only as far as the footlights. Seeing only what was lit up by the lights.

I breathe, you fool, I thought. I live and love and hate. My bare foot—where were my sandals?—hesitated on a jagged pebble and chose a smoother stone. Behind me Lawrence, despite his height and weight, padded easily on his rope-soled espadrilles. But I was leading him. I was the jumping figure in front. I splayed my arms open like a bird and then dropped them again to clutch a sprouting bush. The path had become suddenly steeper. I was completely dry now. The hot sun burnt on my face, dragged at the tendons of my legs which strained to pull me upwards.

I felt the clumsiness of my body, which rocked on its faraway supports. I wanted to fall already on my hands and knees. But we had hardly started to climb. I could see the path stretching narrowly upwards. I knew my body was ungainly to look at. I felt my bottom was pushed out like a tired pregnant woman's. I felt my hips swelling and rolling into ungainly lumps. I didn't know how far Lawrence was behind me but I could imagine

199

him looking lovingly; patronizing my human faults. How he loved humanity!

I stopped for a moment, thought of turning back, confronting him with words. But what could I speak? Besides, I was already half-way to the top and it would be harder to keep a foothold going down than it would be to continue up.

My body was wet again but this time with sweat. It ran intimately, irritatingly down my body. It reminded me suddenly of Emmie and the thought of her sent me on again.

The track got more wavering, dipping suddenly round a rock or a bush so that it almost seemed to disappear down the cliff side. For now we were high above the sea. The sound of the waves was softer than the sound of my breathing. My feet were less and less sure, my toes tried to curl into the ground but instead slid crabwise and sent rattling downwards a drift of pebbles and dust. At some points the track fell away completely and I had to scramble in an arc above its line, clinging uncomfortably to anything that looked at all solid. But the plants hardly had more grip in the dry rubble than I did.

Wearily I dropped to my hands and knees. I couldn't remember why I had started the climb. My feet were stuck with prickles like a pin-cushion and my ankles were scratched and grazed.

'You're not giving up, are you? My proud and fearless creature?' He was shouting from behind me. I had forgotten him for a moment. I must have been going faster than it felt for he still sounded far behind. I pushed myself round, determined to see where he was but equally determined not to lose the tiny patch of sitting space my body had found for itself.

He was standing up, walking with very long slow steps; crossing the chasms I had crawled round with such pain in one extended stride. Then as I watched he sat down. He seemed comfortable on the side of the cliff. His legs sloped downwards relaxedly. He saw me looking and shouted:

'All the best mountain goats take it calmly!' He laughed. 'I'm preserving my tendons for my old age and admiring your speedy progress. You look like some little animal zigzagging up there. But just wait till the old goat catches up with you!'

He was amused at the situation. Treating me as if I was a spoilt child. He would find it tougher going when he reached the point I had. Then he would stop smiling. I rose up on my hands and knees like a runner under starter's orders and looked determinedly ahead.

'She's off!' I heard him cry from behind.

The path was now going almost vertically upwards. If I raised my head, which was difficult in my animal's position, I could see the top of the cliff. I rested once more, panting, nursing my little toe which had caught on a stone and looked more carefully upwards.

'Hell, hell, hell!' I shouted out the words in fury. We were approaching a solid hedge of fat and juicy cactus leaves armoured with spikes like stilettos. 'Hell, hell!' I cried again and only just managed to control my tears. It would be impossible to get through such a determined barrier. Now, too late, I remembered standing on the other side of it when we had parked the car.

'What's that I hear? Swearing from the sweet lips of my lady!' Lawrence was much closer. There were only about ten yards between us. I looked up again despairingly. There wasn't any real path to the cactus hedge even if I could have got through. Only a dried gully half-filled with rubbish, tin cans, cardboard boxes, pieces of wire. All ugly, all certain to slide down the cliff-side if anyone came near. My little path seemed to disappear altogether. Another few yards and it crumbled into nothing.

'We'll certainly have earned our siesta!' He had said that yesterday. In exactly the same voice; in tired but contented anticipation. Probably he would say it again tomorrow, and the next day. He let me plunge and career foolishly around like a horse on a lunging rein while he stood quietly in the middle. Knowing by the end of the day I would be broken again, ready to submit. Except he didn't recognize what was going on, he didn't admit. He didn't see me. His wife was real to him even in his boredom, his friends were real, his job, his house. I was the only one who was special.

I couldn't bear him near me. Scrabbling, clawing, scuffing my toes, scratching my hands, scraping my knees, I started up the gully.

'Ahoy there, Hillary!'

'I'm going to the top.' The words got blocked in my clenched teeth and whistling breath. But I heard him close behind me, coming too. A tin can rattled past me, followed by a flight of old papers like straggly birds. I'll crawl through the stems of the cactus, I was thinking to myself. There's sure to be a bit of space and Lawrence is so much bigger than me he'll never get through. And I'll be the other side right away from him. Already I was in the shade of the massive leaves.

The sun lay the other side and the brightness and cleanness, the golden pillars, the green lizards, and red gladioli. Until that moment I hadn't realized there had been rows of red gladioli. It was all waiting for me the moment I escaped.

'Her husband said what a remarkable bottom and slapped it as hard as he could!'

My body knew it was coming before my mind. He slapped me on the bottom as he would a girl who'd been a good lay, filled an empty night. As he would a sexy secretary who giggled and wore false eye-lashes. As he would any bottom anywhere which took his fancy. It was a hard slap, a cracking good slap which must have been a pleasure to release—like a good sneeze or an orgasm. It hit me fair and square as I burrowed and crawled towards the cactus.

My head went white—light let into a film. I swung round, grasping for support a prickly leaf, I didn't feel the prickles, I saw him for a sharp crack of a moment: he was half-kneeling, hand still outstretched, mouth smiling, chocolate-drop eyes smiling, smiling. Below him the brilliant sea disappeared without a ripple into the sheer cliff-side. He had no foothold, no handhold; only the forward weight of his body against the sliding dirt and rubble stopped him from falling. Still gripping the cactus leaf with one hand, I drew back my left leg and with all the strength in my body, with all my hatred and guilt and love, I kicked him full in his smiling face.

He lost balance immediately. For the first time I saw his limbs lose their usual calm and clumsy grace as they struggled vainly to control his slipping body.

But it was too heavy. His small feet in their soft espadrilles turned upside down and he fell with a drum-roll of tin cans to the bottom of the cliff.

39

*Black bird gone. The sky is as blue and empty as ... black
bird gone. White sun takes the colour from the sky. I
fly. Round and round. Spinning out the colour into white.
Free.*
Free-wheeling.

After all, I couldn't get through the cactus barrier. I
gave up at once when I saw it wasn't possible. But instead I found a slight indentation running round beside it
which gave me enough foothold to circle the promontory. I edged along sideways and after a while I saw the
Lido di Marinello, its pale-washed houses like coloured
beads along the shore.

The cliff was no longer a cliff; it sloped now quite
gently to a sandy beach where two or three little boys
played. Above me was a wire fence and a wall, beyond I
could see the black tarmac road leading to the temples.
I noticed, now, to my surprise, another temple, triumphantly complete on a nearby hill. I thought I would
enjoy driving up to see it closer. But first I had to get
inside the wall.

Then I realized that to my right a bank reached quite
high under the wall so that it would be hard to climb over
it. There was a sort of clean precision in my eye as if
everything I saw was laid out on a map or a *papier
mâché* model. My step was firm. I skirted round the lumps
of carved stone allowed to remain outside the perimeter

of the site. What a wealth of history, I reflected, that one stone more or less made no difference. I started to climb up the bank and over the wall. I noticed then that one of my hands was scratched and bleeding. I looked at it without much sense of how it had happened.

'*Eh! Signorina! Signorina!*'

I hadn't seen the ticket office hidden by the height of the wall. A man, legs sturdily apart, stood on the tarmac and shouted at me. I jumped down calmly into the road. I thought he was a savage peasant and I was a moneyed and educated tourist.

'Ticket,' I said pointing at myself; and then pointing up the road: 'By car.'

He had a dark brown face, prickly with black hairs. He looked puzzled. 'Me swim,' I said flinging my arms in a wide breast stroke, quite certain I would convince him. And indeed now he smiled back at me. 'Very good,' he said, surprising me with yellow stumps of teeth instead of the white five-barred gate I'd assumed. And he began to say something excitedly in Italian. I didn't understand so I shook my head and started to walk away. He shouted again but with no echo of menace, so I didn't look round.

It was slightly cooler now and the colours were much more beautiful. The brilliant sun, which before had drawn the colour from the stones and turned them to a blank white, now in its yellow slanting enriched them with a deep golden yellow. There were the gladioli. Rather absurd in their straight scarlet lines, like rockets on a firing range. I stood over them and touched a petal. Something shuffled round my feet; it was a dog. I patted its smooth back and noticed how the hairs met in a curled ridge. Then, looking along his straight alsatian's nose, I saw some legs. And standing there was a group of men in grey suits with yellow trimmings and fat policemen's hats. For a moment I paused while my fingers, separate, played with the dog's hair. But they were chatting happily to each other; they weren't even looking at me. There was nothing I needed to hide—I was certain of that—nevertheless, I felt vulnerable enough to want the privacy of the car.

It was unchanged under the straw roof. As small and anonymous as ever. I knew it wouldn't be locked because Lawrence had a lazy habit of throwing the key into the glove compartment and slamming the door on responsibility. I opened the door and sat in the driver's seat. The key was immediately obvious, half-pushed into the leaves of the guide book. I felt a wave of habitual irritation at the careless hand that had pushed it there.

I started up the engine and backed slowly away. The cactus hedge, which had been too close to see before, came into focus. For a moment I looked intently at the tangle of grey roots and then I turned the car down the road and sped away. I only regretted there was no wireless in the car to fill my ears with loud music.

I reached the barrier and there was the man who had stopped me before—with a friend. They were smiling so I slowed right down and smiled out of the window, and the original guard slapped the car on the wing as it passed and shouted something after me. 'Goodbye!' I cried in return. 'Goodbye!'

I decided after all not to visit the other temple. In my energy, I didn't want to stop driving. A large arrowed sign suddenly divided the road and I only just remembered to steer to the right of it. It was Marinello again. How drab it looked; how pathetic an imitation of a real sea-side town. No wonder the boys, ever hopeful of escape, gathered round their cars. I pressed my horn to clear the narrow road. Immediately a group of cars fitted snugly round me, front and back, so that I was in the middle of a procession. They were all boys, drivers and passengers twisting and turning in their seats.

Although I was in the middle of the procession, I recognized myself the leader. I stopped outside a *gelati* sign. Opposite, a grey courtyard of tables stared emptily. I would lead the proprietor to his shiny placard and point to the large cornet I coveted. But as I got out I remembered I had no Italian money on me. Two boys approached with their hands in their pockets.

'*Signora!* You wish city?' said the first.

I shook my head and looked away. I was surprised and pleased he had called me *Signora* and assumed it a compliment to my assured independence.

'We good boys,' said his friend, lowering the tone. So I quickly got back into the car. I knew Lawrence had an envelope full of money in his case because he found traveller's cheques too much of a nuisance. But I didn't think this was the moment to look for it. A piece of sun-dried bread would have to fill my stomach.

No wonder I was hungry; it was already six o'clock. I wound my watch hurriedly, suddenly afraid it might stop. I would have to hurry to reach Agrigento before dark, I would, of course, continue our trip round the island. There was never any doubt in my mind about that. I pulled out the guide book and found the route, noticing at the same time that the light seemed dimmer. Till I looked up and saw the pressing bodies round my windows. I bent to put the key back into the ignition and when I straightened up they were drawing back to their own cars. I thought I saw a flash of yellow, the policeman's uniform yellow, but the receding wave of boys blocked my view.

Nevertheless I was the centre of a procession. How small Marinello was. We were through it in a moment. I drove slowly, so we all drove slowly; I was concentrating on a hard stump of bread which needed an immense amount of softening and chewing to make it edible.

I turned right, following the signs to Agrigento and when I looked in my rear-view mirror the procession was shorter at the tail. I smiled at the sense of desertion I felt. I remembered my terror at the boys' snatch and grab techniques in the sea at Palermo. But it seemed a different world. The sense of desertion remained.

I looked again in the mirror and saw my face, calm and pink in the evening sun.

The sun was directly behind me now and the sea was out of sight. I passed through a small town in which dusty streets cut across each other in geometric precision and when I came out the other side there were only two cars at my front and one behind. Then the leader hooted and turned off left. The sun cut across my face through the right-hand window so that, although it wasn't hot any more, I had to put up my hand every now and again to shade my eyes from the light. Then the band of light slipped to my waist until suddenly it was gone. The sky became violet so that the skin of my arm reflected in a marble pallor. I fiddled on the dashboard for some lights and when I found them, hearing the switch click as loud as a door shutting, they lit up a grey empty road. Nor was there anything following.

I started to shiver, frightening myself with the violence of my limbs till I realized I might be cold. The cooling system was still blowing air at my face and neck. I turned it off and the silence was even colder. A cart appeared on the edge of the road. In the daytime it would have seemed brightly painted in whirls and circles but the night reduced all colours to grey and my headlights only brushed it for a moment into light. It seemed to be empty with only an old man riding in front. A little farther on I passed another. This time I noticed a fork and shovel in the back and the horse lit up to a rich chestnut. At the side of the road a twittering noise began, coming quite clearly through my open window. It was the cicadas singing for me as I passed. Soon there was another cart and another, all trotting along at the end of the day. The noses of the horses were lifted as if they were eager to be home.

We must be coming to a town. I was tired, too, and the car had very little petrol. There were no more carts now but I could see lights ahead.

'Sciacca.' New blocks of flats enclosed the town. I drove on looking for the centre and by the salty smell in the air realized I was on the sea again. Now once again I was surrounded by the noisy motor bikes and little white cars, pushing by in the narrow road, but now as if night had made me invisible, no one looked my way or hooted or shored me up, front and back.

It was a big town and the road I drove along was impressively lined with trees and global lamps. Then, to my right, a raised and cobbled square opened out. Beyond it spread a wide arch of black sky and I could imagine the sea far below. I stopped the car under one of the lamps.

I meant to get out my coat from the boot till I felt the air, now I was no longer moving, as soft and warm as a shawl. So only by chance I remembered to open Lawrence's case to search for money. I had unpacked it that morning so I knew exactly where the envelope was. I took out two five-hundred-lire notes and then thoughtfully chose a large five-thousand note. I shut the case firmly.

As I had thought, the square ended at the sea but instead of a direct drop, there was a gradual slope built up with houses and roads. To my left, however, I guessed it fell more dramatically. That part seemed to belong to a café. The lights were dim, but I could see a few wooden tables surrounded by men in dark trousers and jackets.

I thought of coffee with longing and instead of strolling, walked decisively.

'*Signora?*' The waiter was very small and neat with a white jacket. The men at the table, I noticed, were old or middle-aged. The waiter didn't exactly block my path but he wasn't welcoming me either. My tiredness made it easier to be obtuse.

'Coffee,' I said, crossing determinedly to a free table near a curving stone parapet. No one spoke on the terrace and everybody looked. But I found the attention surprisingly reassuring after the loneliness of the night countryside. I wondered vaguely if I had trespassed into a men's club and then repeated 'coffee' more loudly. White shoulders shrugged and he disappeared.

I wandered to the parapet. I passed close to a group of five or six men. They looked down as I passed. It made me smile. They had a bottle of red wine and some heavy crude-cut glasses.

I leant over the parapet and heard the talk begin again behind me. The sea below was too far away to be of any significance. I sighed and turned back.

The waiter was bringing my coffee to the table.

'*Vino,*' I said.

He shrugged. '*Rosso?*'

'Sì.'

He flapped the tin tray against his thigh and dipped away. I felt triumphant with my first conversation.

'Hotel?' I said when he returned. But he only slapped down the bill and said, '*Quattrocento.*' As if he wanted to settle up with me and forget my existence. He took my five-hundred note and hurried away. I didn't want to travel any further tonight. I poured out the wine. Even the smell made me dizzy with delight. I drank and poured out another glass and my head became deliciously separated from my body.

When I stood up the bottle fell over but only the smallest trickle of wine curled slowly out. I watched it soak into the wood-topped table and then turned away.

I played a game with myself across the wide space of cobbles. I was a pawn, or a draught, or a boot or a galleon, full rigged ... I tittered to myself. At any rate I was on my board, finding my path, in the game, eager to win ... I zigzagged towards the car, throwing imaginary dice, advancing and retreating. My aim was so good that I had actually run quite heavily into the car before I could stop myself. My bare feet rocked on the kerb.

'The winner!' I cried.

I got into the unlocked car and with some difficulty pushed myself across to the driving seat. 'Conclusively, the winner,' I mumbled, head nodding.

'You want hotel, *signora?*' I rolled my head backwards. I wasn't sure whether the voice was inside my head or outside.

A face spoke again at the window. My heart flapped emptily with sudden fear. Then it took courage again. It was the waiter, his little white coat replaced by a sharp navy blue blazer. I laughed patronizingly.

He seemed to take that as assent and climbed quickly into the seat beside me.

'I show good hotel.'

'Good!' I replied fumbling with the ignition key. I concentrated enough to turn switches and knobs and found that it started up my mind as well as the car. We drove along the lighted main street and I glanced sideways at the man beside me. Would he lunge at me, I wondered, as I got out of the car, or after he had shown me the hotel, if there was a hotel?

'*A sinistra*,' he said, pointing left, in an efficiently cold voice which rather surprised me. There was a kind of respectful formality where there had been only disapproval before. But he didn't convince me. He must have decided for one reason or another I was worth playing along. The point was whether I should play him along until he showed me the hotel or whether I should stop the car now and push him out. I flicked another quick look sideways; he was very small. It really was a question of the existence of the hotel: true or false.

'Hotel *grande*?' I said probingly.

'*Simpaticissimo ... cucina casalinga ... con tutti i conforti ...*' I picked up a few words as he burst into a hand-waving parade of assets. It convinced me to carry on further although, looking at the narrowness of the street with yellow sandstone buildings leaning cosily towards each other separated every few yards by uneven steps angling steeply upwards, I could hardly believe the hotel would be big.

'*Ecco arrivati.*' His staccato command reminded me of my driving instructor and I found myself doing an emergency stop. The waiter, naturally unprepared, fell forward sharply and hit his head on the windscreen. I

thought this is it, now's your moment, throw him out...
But instead I laughed. He held his head and looked round
at me reproachfully. I could discover no lurking passion
in his small dark eyes.

'I'm terribly sorry,' I said. 'You see, you reminded me
of my driving instructor in England and I always was
rather good at emergency stops.' Gaining momentum
from my story, I raised my eyebrows and spread my
hands and cried, 'Hit me, if you like! Go on, hit me!'

He looked surprised at my tone of voice and got quickly
out of the car. I scrambled after him. He dived into a dark
and narrow entrance. I dived after him.

'Wait! Wait for me!' We ran up two flights of stairs,
one behind the other and I stopped shouting because I
was out of breath. I had decided not to chase him any
further when I reached a landing with a desk on it. My
waiter leant against it familiarly.

'*Pensione Moderno*,' he said, '... *mio fratello*.' Another
man, with red hair, stood behind the desk. Hanging round
the desk were flags from various countries.

'Very good,' said his brother with red hair. I panted.

'Oh, yes,' said the waiter with deep feeling. 'Most
good.'

'Good,' I repeated, recovering a little.

'Baggage?' enquired the proprietor politely. The waiter
clapped him on the shoulder and ran down the stairs
again.

'Oh, no,' I thought. Left alone with my small dark
room. I had expected to be chased into it.

The room, as it happened, turned out to be very big. It
must have been the second floor salon belonging to a
great house. Now it held four beds, one large enough for
three English bodies, five Italians. I lay across it. A small

213

bunch of plastic violets was suspended in a cornet above the big bed head. On the other wall there was an ebony cross, heavily carved with fruits and flowers.

Lawrence's case lay, like mine, on the smallest bed, almost a cot. The obvious masculinity of its heavy leather must have seemed odd to the Italians. I took off my dress and opened the lid. It was immediately obvious that someone had been through it. The envelope from which I had taken the money earlier, lay on the top. Now quite empty. It seemed odd to me that a thief with the whole car to search had made such a direct hit. I had not been at the café long.

I went back to the great bed and lay down again. The exhilaration from the wine had passed away leaving me lifeless. Now, I thought, as I lie here drained and empty, with no money, no person, not even an Italian to chase me, now I will find out what I really am. Then, with a sudden vividness that startled me, I realized how closely, in my sprawled position, limbs thrown unregarded open, I must resemble him, Lawrence, at the bottom of the cliff. It seemed the most exquisite justice. I realized I had been waiting for this moment to think of him. My trip round the island was a tribute to him. The idea filled me with content. I switched off the light by pressing a button which swung above my head. When I let it go it bounced against the wall in a gradually lessening cadence of knocks. By the time it hung still, the memory of a body had faded and I was curled under the bedclothes into a tight coil of dreamless sleep.

40

A knocking woke me up again in the morning. Although this time it was from outside the room. Ears, nose and eyes immediately filled with a thousand sensations. The whole street seemed to be pressing through my half-open shutters: horses, lorries, boys, bells, women gossiping, scooters revving and harsh cries of men selling their produce. I couldn't think how I had slept through it all. I leapt out of bed and flung open the door.

'*Permesso, signorina. E pronto la colazione. Caffelatte, panini . . .*' said a humble woman in black.

'*Sì. Sì. Sì.*' I was immensely hungry. I pushed past her to the bathroom and was almost overwhelmed by the smell. The bath was filled with silver swimming fish. I dabbled my fingers light-heartedly in the water and watched them flicker away in terror. Doubtless they were there for a very good reason.

Back in my room the sun was so warm and cheerful on the floor that I wanted to curl up and smile like a china cat. Instead I chose a dress and shoes and rushed for my breakfast. It was served in a tiled room which reminded me of a smart hotel lavatory with a few hygienic potted plants and a lot of white linen. The humble black woman hovered eagerly with stewed fruit and toasted bread rolls. It was as if the night before had split open revealing a brilliant lining. I kept smiling at the woman whom I now saw was quite young with smooth rosy skin and after a bit she smiled too, wrinkling her skin cheerfully round her eyes and ears. There was no one else in the room. At length our smiles became so conspiratorial and intimate that one of us had to speak. She took the plunge, pointing at me a rather crooked finger with short cut nails:

'Husband?' she said in English. I noticed a gold tooth in the back of her mouth. She stood back excitedly to wait for the answer.

'Oh, no,' I said vigorously, shaking my head. 'I not like men. Oh, no. Not at all.' And I made a face of disgust.

This sent her into a wave of suppressed laughter and her eyes gleamed understandingly. She pointed her finger again and spoke though barely able to produce the word through her laughter.

'*Bambini?*' she said. '*Bambini?*'

'*Bambini!*' I cried, carried away with the success of my performance. 'Horrible! Terrible! Smellee! Nastee!' I contorted my face into the most horrific look of nausea and then flung my eyes to heaven. '*Bambini* ruin a woman's life!' She can't have understood me, nevertheless she clutched her bosom with delight at my acting and herself poured out a string of excited thoughts on the subject, which unfortunately I couldn't understand. When she had finished for the moment—signified by crossing her hands and clucking with an expression of satisfaction—I took over again and tipping my chair backwards cried:

'Just think how delightful life would be without a man to work for! Just look at yourself, pretty, gay, young and spending your time slaving in the kitchen, dressed in black and producing children! All to please the ego of your husband . . .' How true it all seemed to me. For a moment I even imagined snatching her away from her spotless linen and driving her off in my car. But at this point she gave a sudden nervous squeak and, grabbing my empty bowl of fruit, scuttled out of the room.

'It is good?'

The ego of her husband, the red hair, and we were back to the scintillating conversation of the night before, though now it seemed more belligerent.

'Oh, yes,' I said eagerly, hopeful of making up for any marital problems I had caused. 'Very, very good.'

'Check, yes?' He stood slightly behind me so I had to swivel uncomfortably and strain my neck. I felt there was little choice in the question of the bill.

'Thank you.' He laid a neatly folded piece of white paper beside my plate and stood back waiting. I picked it up. It was two thousand five hundred. I handed him my five-thousand note. It had seemed a lot when I took it from the case. My change would hardly pay for petrol. Yet the car was vital to me. I could only just see it when I got to the bottom of the stone steps. No one had offered to carry my cases so I was weighted down with one on either side. I let them go on the pavement. One case fell over. About twenty boys were gathered round the car, draped across the bonnet, drooping along the bumpers, even one cross-legged on the roof. He was the only one to move at my appearance and that, I'm sure, was in order to give me a better view of his lissom figure. I thought, here we are, battle is joined!

'Hoy!' I shouted as a preliminary. 'You can't do that. That's my car.' I threw back my hair defiantly, feeling the immense heat buoying up my body like a hot bath.

'Oh, miss!' a wheedling voice clothed in a slim brown face and yellow shirt, picked up my cases for me and stared into my face. I stared back noticing his nose was crooked. 'Oh, miss, *mi dispiace*, we like car, very beautiful car. Very beautiful girl.' I began to laugh and like imitative children they laughed too. I pushed my way to the car and unlocked the door. I heaved the two cases on to the back seat and was conscious as I did so that my skirt would have cleared my thighs. But when I brought my head out again the group of boys had moved back. Some were quietly going to their cars but others were just staring vacantly. I couldn't understand why they had left me. Then I saw the red-headed owner of the *pensione* leaning, arms crossed, against the wall. He seemed to be standing sentinel and I immediately guessed he had warned off the boys. I wondered vaguely why he had bothered, since his behaviour inside the *pensione* had been hardly friendly. I felt a sense of anti-climax.

There was nothing else to do but to start up the car and drive out of the town. I hooted my horn and waved cheerfully. The boys in their cars shouted and waved back. My spirits rose again.

In the daylight the town was bigger than I had imagined. There was time to remember what traffic was like again, to stare idiotically at signs while a train of cars built up behind, to be glad when I saw the unmistakable arrow for Agrigento, when at length I broke through into the waves of golden cornfields. This part of Sicily seemed much more pastoral than the barren west.

In a way I missed the drama.

Not that I didn't have plenty to think about: my financial situation, for example; 'I have one thousand lire left and the car is full of petrol.' Although I spoke out loud it didn't make the observation seem any more significant. I tried to put it another way: 'I can drive to Syracuse and eat perhaps one loaf of bread and drink, with luck, a bottle of wine—the bottled sort that's slightly fizzy and turns a brown colour in the heat.' That certainly made it seem more real. 'That is very interesting,' I said aloud. 'And in my case and my companion's case I have several saleable items: item, one electric shaver, unused, packed by loving wife against less loving husband's wishes. Item, one good suit, in slightly outdated style and rather too large a size for most Sicilian snappy dressers but nevertheless a fine piece of cloth. Item, one pair handmade shoes with carved wood shoe-horns, a collector's piece complete with original toe imprints of well-known London and international publisher.' Liking the sound of my pure English voice, well-modulated, well-educated, I would have gone on with the list but I noticed my Fiat followers were getting restless with my slow pace. A car came alongside with a boy hanging out of the windows, back and front. 'Sorry!' I shouted, putting my foot on the accelerator. And they shouted something jovial in return which I didn't understand.

I think they expected me to stop when I arrived at Agrigento or at least to visit the temple ruins. For the cars in front of me turned off the highway to the town centre at the yellow tourist signs for the site. But I was enjoying my drive and had no intention of losing my momentum. I hooted my horn to the cars behind me but they turned off anyway. So I pulled up. I wanted to look at the map. 'Licata', 'Gela', there didn't seem to be any very big towns on my route, unless I left the coast and turned to the hot inland regions. I remembered pictures of the mosaics at Piazza Armerina, but I couldn't remember if they had been on our itinerary. I knew that Syracuse was. I had high hopes of Syracuse. The very name was enough to lure me forward. I remembered even Lawrence had been enthusiastic about Syracuse. He had said the harbour was the most beautiful he had ever seen and even the sailors were romantics. I didn't believe the bit about the sailors but I loved the idea of the wide golden harbour with a fleet of white sails waiting to put to sea.

I sat in the car considering this happy thought and when I started again I had collected a new escort of cars. One driver had a startlingly brilliant turquoise shirt which reminded me how drab I must look. They wouldn't stay long if I didn't improve my appearance. After all, the English had a reputation for being the swinging centre of the rag trade and here was I in an outpost of the civilized world, sporting a dirty creased dress and not wearing a scrap of make-up. I would have to stop soon and give myself a lick and a polish. In fact at that very moment I could see in my rear mirror a boy combing his shiny black hair with intense concentration. He had a little pocket mirror which he was holding between his teeth.

'Gosh! I'm sorry!' No one heard me speak but I had only just avoided running into the car in front. It had slowed down suddenly before a great pothole in the road. I bumped over it and the movement in my stomach reminded me of my food. The car in front had parked at the side of the road so I stopped beside it, got out and went over to the window. My dress stuck to the back of my thighs.

'Restaurant,' I said. The two boys in the car looked at each other and I was surprised they didn't get out. Relieved, of course. '*Ristorante.*' One of the two, his turquoise shirt on closer inspection was made of an unattractive shiny material, began to speak energetically.

'*Lento,*' I said, flapping my hand, but he looked blank and his companion shrugged his shoulders. Suddenly octopus-like fingers reaching from behind me coiled round my upper arm. I swung round and the hand fell away at once. It belonged to the first fat Sicilian boy I had seen with round oily features and shirt open to the waist. His chest was hairless which struck me as odd in this Latin country. He licked his lips. His manner reminded me of a nervous television interviewer.

'You English?' he said with some difficulty.

'Oh, yes,' I replied eagerly, discounting his appearance. 'How marvellous, you speak English! You can help me so much. I'm having so much trouble in getting people to help me. There's so much I want to ask, though I suppose top priority just at the moment is to get something to eat. Do you know somewhere? Quite ordinary, I mean. Bread or anything will do. It would be marvellous!'

A friend had joined the fat boy while I was talking and seemed to be drawing him away from me. I said again excitedly:

'It would be wonderful really, if you could help!'

The fat boy shook off his friend who was definitely trying to hold him back and took up his stance again in front of me. I waited, as it were with the mike, expectantly.

'I speak English.' He licked his lips in triumph.

I was relieved at this reaffirmation but a little impatient.

'Yes. Yes. I know. It's awfully clever of you. I only wish I spoke Italian. The trouble is England thought it was the master race when I grew up, so we weren't taught much languages and besides, I personally never had much of an ear. However, that's not the point now. The point is whether you could help me find something to eat?'

He stared at me blankly, but I was sure behind his

stupid small eyes great sentences of information were forming. Quite a group of boys had collected behind him now, but none of them came very close so I didn't have to worry.

I thought perhaps my grammar had been a little involved and began again:

'Eat,' I pointed to my mouth. But at this simple mime several of the boys began to laugh convulsively and without any warning the car behind me moved away. I had been half leaning against it so I nearly fell backwards into the space it left. And when I had righted myself and looked up again all the boys were going off.

'Wait!' I cried.

But even the fat boy got back into his car.

'Stop! Please, stop!'

I was alone once more. I looked round me. We had pulled up beside a piece of rough uncultivated land which grew nothing, gave food for nothing. I walked a little way and when my back was turned, another car passed but so quickly that I had no time for a clear view of it. But it seemed bigger than the usual pocket Fiat.

Oh, well. I pushed back my hair from my face. I supposed I would find some restaurant in the next town even without their help. I got into my car disconsolately. It had become very hot through standing still in the midday sun and for a moment I thought I might even black out. But of course it was hunger. I started up the engine again.

My road went through Licata, but although I drove very slowly I couldn't see any shops open. It was about half past two, so presumably everyone was busy with lunch and siesta. The pavements were empty, the rows of brilliant plastic buckets and basins and balls and brushes

222

unattended. I supposed I had lost my escort also to this blank middle of the day. I thought how nice it would be to stretch in the sun. So when after the town the sea came up close to the road I stopped the car and lay down on the verge. The waves were near enough to hear but being almost tideless there was only the gentlest swish as they broke. I didn't fall asleep. I found the very silence began to make its own sharp disturbances of flying things and crawling things that twitched the dry grass and seemed to threaten my bare legs. The earth under me was as hard and unwelcoming as floorboards. I wondered sadly who had stolen my money. A car passed. Two nuns sat in the front and three in the back. They wore black headdresses which were flowing in the wind.

I sat up hurriedly and pulled down my skirt. 'Excuse me, sisters,' I spoke to myself as they disappeared into a distant blue, 'I am English and I have had an unfortunate experience. I fear you may not wish to speak to me when you hear my tale.' I shook my head. That's not what I thought at all. I was quite certain they would praise my behaviour with heavenly alleluias. That is, if they were at all intelligent. For a flash I saw Lawrence's smiling red lips. I rolled over onto my stomach. 'Sisters,' I began again, but with more strength and conviction in my voice, for after all death to them is the most joyous of gifts ... the True Life. 'Sisters, dear ...' I picked a blade of grass which still kept a touch of juice at its root and sucked it thoughtfully. 'The behaviour of certain young people ... It has been brought to my notice ...' I got up slowly and wandered back to the car, which this time I had sensibly put into the shade of a hard little tree.

After a while another car came by. It slowed down as it reached me and a boy with a smooth black fringe stared

223

out at me. I smiled back guilelessly.

Then, to my surprise, he wound up his window and passed by. I jumped into my car, turned on the engine and started after him. It was time to move. The air was cooler. But I couldn't keep pace with the car in front. The road had left the sea and become quite winding. He screeched round the bends as if he was in a race. So I lost him.

Luckily it wasn't very far to the next town, Gela. It was again set on a hill above the sea. I found the main street easily and noticed with relief the shops were now open. I parked the car by a surprisingly modern church which lay back from a great square. My legs felt quite weak when I got out of the car. I looked rather dazedly at the people filling the streets. They all seemed much bigger than I had remembered. The women, particularly, were coated with rolls of hard flesh. There were tables in the square, so I sat down quickly and was immediately faced by a waiter barely three feet high. I stared at him stupidly. He wore a striped tee-shirt with 'Yankee' stencilled across it and a yellow yachting cap; a white apron trailed round his ankles. He was just a little boy.

'Two coffees,' I said clearing my throat.

'Yankee,' he replied proudly, making no move to take my order.

'Coffee,' I insisted, stretching my mouth. And at last he ran across the road to where the café was.

The sun came to me in spots of light through a flowered sunshade which leant rakishly over the table. I sat back in my chair which was laced with yellow plastic thongs and admitted that I would have liked a companion. Not a desperate need, but a feeling that it would go well with the coffee. The coffee was so strong that I gripped the sides of my chair as it hit my stomach. The painted flowers above my head danced. I went across to the café to find a lavatory. It was a small bar with a silent juke box. Before I could say anything a large man in a dirty apron pointed to a door. The lavatory smelt and made me feel even odder than the coffee had. I bought a Perugina chocolate at the bar and walked out again into the sun. I felt too dizzy to wander about, so I went back to my car.

It was now entirely surrounded by other parked cars. I got into it but it was obvious I couldn't move it unless the car directly behind me was moved. I got out and looked around hopelessly. There were quite a lot of people in the square but no one was interested. I looked at the car blocking my way. It had a dog hanging on the windscreen with green glass eyes that glittered. I went up closer and peered at it. The black satin nose and scarlet mouth were meticulously embroidered on its face. With sudden determination I went back to my own car and put my arm through the open window. My hand could just reach the horn. I looked round at the square and the street and the people and pressed it as hard as I could. The noise was an immediate answering shriek. Instinctively I relaxed the pressure. But among the people in the square only two had turned their heads and then only for a passing second. The shriek continued in my head. I pressed my hand down again. The horn wailed protestingly louder and louder. I leant my body against the car and opening my mouth wide screamed in unison.

A man had been standing watching me from a low brick wall. Half unconsciously I had been watching him too. He looked like an English lorry driver. Now he slowly detached himself from the wall, crossed the road and came towards me. It was as if he had been waiting for some command which he had now received. I closed my mouth and waited for him. But his orders didn't include conversation, for he passed me by in silence and went to the car which was blocking my way. Very casually he opened the door and backed it off.

No one came near me. There was only the empty space where his car had been. The square was exactly as it had been before except, perhaps as I raised my eyes wearily there were more young girls. Three passed now on the edge of the square, arms linked like school girls in a crocodile. I started forward to see them more clearly. How smart they were! Leather handbags slung across their olive arms, leather shoes matching their handbags, both as shiny as new chestnuts. And their hair brushed into sculptured waves of light and shadow. The girl in the middle had painted in a few golden highlights. I had almost forgotten the existence of such confidence, such elegance. It seemed so long ago that I had been a part of it, walking with the sleek rod of Emmie beside me. I considered the thought for a moment, then pulled at my crumpled dress and stepped forward determinedly. My hand tapped the arms of the girl who stood on the right-hand side.

'Excuse me. I wonder if you could help me...' My voice broke nervously.

She looked at her friend and giggled. She didn't look at me at all. Nor did they slow their pace. I was half running in my awkward twisted position to speak to their faces. Nevertheless, I persevered. I appealed to the girl with the blonde streak as the most sophisticated of the trio; 'Could you stop for a moment...?' I pressed forward. They were talking to each other in shuffling kinds of undertones like nuns telling their beads. Now we were out of the square and along a broad main street. People started coming towards us so there was no room on the pavement for me. I slipped off once and then again and it seemed to me that the outer girl was tripping me off with her shiny toe. Desperately, I tried to block their path; I fell into the street again. 'But you don't understand ... You don't understand!' I wailed. I looked imploringly at their eyes —as black and clear as new tar—and they looked away from me; the white of their eyes was as pure as the white of an egg. And I understood they could never see me with those eyes.

I gave up, fell behind and my shoes scuffed in the dust. A few yards further on they stopped too and turned round to stare. It was as if at a distance, as an object, I came into focus. Breaking into a run, swinging my arms so that they warded off other pedestrians, I fled back to the car.

41

I was driving east to Syracuse. The road which was always empty and black could have been the same stretch over and over again. On either side golden cornfields rose to the horizon.

When night fell I drove the car down a little dirt track which appeared suddenly on my left. In the fading light the endless corn became a dark bronze shroud all around until I saw green below me, for the track dipped steeply downwards. It seemed to be going to a dried river-bed. The car bumped over some stones and my eyes which had been almost closed, jerked open. The car stopped or perhaps I stopped it. The track had become very narrow, I wandered down it. The green, nearly black in the night, grew high in waving bushes. The rutted track sank lower and became overhung with banks. One tree appeared to be covered in scarlet flowers, now almost blood-coloured, another had long slender leaves which glistened faintly. A third, with large leaves shaped like flattened hands, I recognized as a fig tree.

Then to my left, a solid wall of smooth stone rose up. I looked at it wonderingly. It was convex to me like a spoon turning its back and yet there was something manufactured about it. Then I saw a step carved into it and another higher up; and far above my head in the dark of the trees that overshadowed it, I thought I could see a hole.

I took off my shoes and put my feet into the first step. There was nothing to hold on to. I sprang up and swung myself flat against the pearly stone. It was smooth and cool against my hot cheeks. I reached for the next step with my fingers and then threw up my leg as high as it would go. My toes curled neatly into the niche. I kept in front of me the picture of that black hole above. When I reached it in reality, I believe my eyes were shut, yet I could see it quite clearly. One foot and then the other slid into it and then my whole body. I fell onto the earthy floor which was soft and warm and went to sleep.

42

I was in the sunlight driving very fast. The car had almost run out of petrol and the next town was still several kilometres. My back was very stiff and to ease it I had pushed my seat very close to the wheel. My feet were flaccid at the end of my legs. It was an effort to press the brake.

I put my head out of a deep black hole lined with soft brown earth and fringed with flowering trees ... Below me was a track and growing under the trees a line of healthy tomato plants. I had fallen out of the smooth stone and bruised my back on the track as I fell. The pain brought me into sharp consciousness. The bright sun came speckled through the pointed leaves. Down the track further away from the road I heard someone digging and whistling as he dug. There was also a faint wisp of smoke carrying with it the smell of sweet wood. I walked briskly towards my car. The door was open as I had left it the night before. It smelt strongly of the sour cheese which was still lying on the back seat and the drying salami. Nevertheless I was hungry enough to eat a few curling slices.

The road shimmered under my eyes. I had the map spread on the seat beside me so I knew how much further it was to Syracuse. The road I was taking went round most of the villages and towns. But I would stop in the next one which was called Florida. That amused me. But when I arrived there it turned out to be called Floridia. Nevertheless I filled the car with petrol and was left with a hundred and fifty lire.

But I wasn't in the least worried. I had remembered about the Hotel Politi. It was a beautiful hotel on the sea just outside Syracuse. Winston Churchill had stayed there in a suite of front rooms. There was a brochure describing it, stuck in the pages of the guide. It was the grand climax of our trip. We were booked in there. All the best rooms had balconies and there was a lovely porticoed terrace set with pink tables. The service was immaculate. You would think you were in the south of France. It was quite something to look forward to. I brushed away a crumb of loose earth which had gathered in my lap. It must have fallen from my hair.

An avenue of dark fir trees led up to Syracuse. I had hardly seen the sign Syracuse before I saw 'Villa Politi', written up in white on a blue background. There was a sign at every turn in the road as if I was being given personal guidance. I seemed to skirt the town for I soon found myself close to the sea shore above which bushes, hanging with red-bellied flowers, grew in wild liberality. I followed the blue sign left into a small square and up a little hill. There it was, at last, though I hadn't been impatient or bored. The entrance lay between two carved stone pillars, through a garden, so green and thickly grown it reminded me of England, and the villa was in front of me.

I joined a few other cars under a sweep of stone stairs, like a smile curved downwards across the wide stone building. I got out of the car and looked upwards. Eagerly I studied the carved balconies, the bow-fronted wings, the balustraded terrace I had read about. My impatience to arrive which had been growing through the long drive, could not be settled at once. A porter came running down the right-hand sweep of the steps. I jumped back to let him pass. But he stopped in front of me.

'You have baggage, *signora?*' he bowed deferentially. Indeed I had arrived. My back straightened. My head lifted.

'Yes,' I said, joyfully, 'in the back of the car.' I wandered up the way he had come down. The steps passed through the terrace; I looked up and there were the looped garlands of globe lamps; I looked down and there were the rows of little tables covered with pink cloths. A waiter was putting round ashtrays.

'Good evening.' I said, and then rushing to continue the conversation. 'I'll have a drink down here later. When it's twilight.'

'*Sì, signora,*' he said politely, and unloaded his last ashtray.

The villa was just as impressive inside. I gazed round at the great hall of wood panelling, like a Scottish baronial castle. And the stained-glass windows and the dark oak furniture and the massive fireplace.

'You wish a room, *signora?*'

The desk clerk was tall and distinguished.

'It's booked,' I said, 'Mrs Mann.'

'Oh, yes. Mrs Mann. Of course. You have baggage?'

'He's bringing it in,' I said, leaning my elbows on the counter. 'Is my husband here yet?'

But he had turned away to receive my porter who was struggling to do up one of the clasps on my case which had come undone. They both bent over it while I waited.

'Room 121,' the desk clerk said eventually, straightening up. The porter started away and I began to follow him until I suddenly had a thought and doubled back.

'I'm just going for a stroll,' I said, passing the clerk when he didn't look up. Why hadn't he asked for my passport? Surely that was normal procedure. I would stay outside for a few moments and then pass him once more. Down the stone steps again. To the left was a low stone wall. I leant my elbows on it as I had on the desk in the hall. The sun which was sinking behind my back gently warmed my shoulders. I looked down and saw a great rocky hole, grown about with heavy green bushes. An old quarry. At the bottom it was flat and some seats were laid out as if for a concert. The sun's rays passed over it making it seem black and cold in contrast to the still brilliant landscape all round. Beyond was the sea, blue and glittering; above it the hotel's garden sparkling with coloured flowers. I stood in the sun and looked down.

'April!' It was my name whispering up from the depths of the pit to where I stood on the brink. 'April!' There was someone down there certainly. But my name ... I was too sensible to believe it really was my name being called out. I knew how sound distorts and how another person standing in my place would have heard their name quietly coming through the bushes.

I leant further over the balustrade and tried to see beyond the flat base into the wooded paths.

Was that a shadow crossing a path down there? But how could there be shadow with no sun? I took my elbows off the parapet and rubbed them. I had been leaning on them so hard they were quite sore.

'April!'

I refused to look this time. I turned round briskly and went into the hotel.

'Will you find your room all right, Mrs Mann?' said the

clerk. 'Or shall I come to show it?'

'I'll find it.' I walked up the wide oak stairs letting my hand slide along the banisters. The feel of the old smooth wood under my fingers calmed me. Room one hundred and twenty-one. The door was slightly ajar. I stepped through it into a little ante room, on one side a bathroom, on the other a cupboard. I couldn't yet see the actual bedroom.

'Close the door, my sweet, would you, or the windows will smash to.'

'Sorry,' I said, going obediently to the door.

'Now come back here.' Lawrence lay on the bed, head raised on one elbow. He only wore jeans and his bare feet were crossed at the ankles. He patted a space on the bed beside his belly.

'What were you doing?' he said. I went past him to the windows. The flimsy white curtains blew in towards my face. I turned into the room again so that I became a black silhouette against the reddening sky.

'You were magnificent,' he said, more humbly. 'So magnificent when you pushed me. I fell, you know, quite a long way. What did you want, my darling?'

He sighed, and the curtains behind me brushed across my hair.

'Did you want to kill me?'

I watched as he brought up his arms and put them behind his head so they encircled his face like a picture frame. The skin on the inside of his arms was pale and tender-looking. His face by contrast seemed immensely used and old. He put a hand across his face defensively. I turned my eyes away. 'Did you love me so much?' His voice was weary. 'My golden creature.' I turned my back on him and stepped onto the balcony. It was dusk; the

234

saddest time of the day. I came in; closed the windows and stood at the end of Lawrence's bed.

'Don't accuse me now. I know. I know.' His arm still shielded his face. He spoke low. 'Did you really want to kill me?'

I sat down beside him on the edge of the bed. He raised himself a little and touched my arm. I drew it back.

'You had a very good try, you know. I've got a beautiful collection of bruises, just turning a rich colour now.'

He smiled slightly but I looked down seriously at his chest and arms. The skin was patterned with green and purple and jagged crimson patches.

'Look at my hands,' he said. On the back of his left hand there was a long partly healed scratch and the palm of his right was indented with red welts. I touched it lightly.

'What brutality.' He didn't smile now. 'And afterwards, my darling, my love, afterwards what bravery. All those terrible places you stayed in. Did you think of me? Or did you picture me safe at the bottom of the cliff? Did you think of me?'

I got up again and went over to the wardrobe. I opened it. Only my lost sandals, neatly side by side. I looked down at our two suitcases side by side on the floor. As innocuous now as they had been at the beginning of the journey. As disparate.

'So much to say and you're so tired. I did admire you. I didn't think you would keep going so long. No money. No language. No friends. I did admire you.' He half roused himself and switched on the bedside light beside him. 'Or were you acting, my love? Did you know I was there, following you, watching over you? Is that why you could do it?'

I sat down on an upright chair by a table. I laid my

arms on its smooth surface.

'But I don't believe you did. I believe you thought I was dead—until yesterday. You found out, then, didn't you?'

I laid my head into my arms.

'Are you sleeping, my darling. my baby, my brave one? Are you sleeping? Like a child, like a child.'

I lifted my head and stared at him silently.

'But you can't pretend any more. Can you? Did you know I was there? Did you know. Did you know?'

We sat at a pink table along the terrace. I had my hand on the tablecloth and Lawrence put his hand on top of it. I looked at it and let it lie there. We had drinks with ice. I was washed and clear-skinned. Lawrence was still talking:

'. . . . I wanted to know so much what was in your head. I've never known that. I used to get sudden moments, little glimpses, but that was all. When you came to my office, do you remember, and then you ran away. I didn't want to probe, I didn't think it was my right . . . and you didn't ask about me. Sometimes I wanted to cut your head open like an apple and look for the core. When your sister died. Not even then.'

The waiter I had spoken to earlier was moving along the terrace towards us. He stopped at each table and, deferentially, back bowed, noted down orders. Vacantly, I watched his progress.

'You didn't say anything to me. Did you to other people? I don't think so. Then, I thought you did, now I think not. Have you ever talked to anyone, April? Did you hear me calling you? April! April! You thought I was in the quarry, didn't you? I wasn't. I was standing on the balcony of my room. Have you ever shown yourself to anyone, April? You hadn't, had you? Never, Never. With me you had an excuse not to. Didn't you? I was married. Everything was secret.'

The waiter now approached our table but before he could attract Lawrence's attention I smiled at him and shook my head. He passed by.

'Why, April? Why? Were you so afraid of what might come out? So afraid? But when your sister died it became too difficult suddenly, didn't it? Or not so necessary, after all? Was that it? Was it your sister? Were you so in awe of her? Was she so perfect? Were you so insignificant by her side? All those great defences built to protect yourself against her and then she dies. Did you feel you'd killed her? My darling! My darling! My poor darling!'

The terrace was dark, lit only by a few globe lamps which gave a pale yellow glow like a row of summer moons. The air was so soft that it seemed to stroke my skin. My hand was still under his.

'No,' I said very quietly, without taking it away. 'No.' Our chairs were almost side by side against the wall of the hotel so it was difficult for Lawrence to see my face. I turned round to him. He sighed and his voice began again. But the excitement had gone from it.

'Well, it's all right now, isn't it? You made it real. You broke through. What a weight you had been bearing. When I followed you, when I watched you, you were like a sleepwalker and I was afraid to wake you up. And after all, I thought, I knew you would come to me.' He laughed a bit. 'I left you no choice anyway when I took the money. I knew you'd come here.' He put his elbows on the table and, taking up his empty glass, dangled it between his fingers. 'I'm sorry you wanted to kill me, my darling. Sorry for myself, I mean. Not for you. I'm glad for you. You're free now, aren't you? And that means you won't want me any more. Of course, I know that. I accept that. But I can't help feeling sorry for myself.'

We lay side by side in our separate beds, but our hands were still joined across the space between us. The light was switched off but we had opened the curtains so that a shadowy reflection of the moonlit sky filled the room. I lay on my back and Lawrence lay turned on his side towards me. He was still talking:

'Did you ever doubt that you pushed me? You mustn't ever doubt that. I should have fallen to the bottom. I had a hard time persuading the police not to pick you up. Without Enrico and Emmie rolling her eyes I would never have done it.' He paused and a deep silence filled the room. 'She wasn't very important...'

A car came roaring up the driveway. Its yellow headlamps flashed across the ceiling. Doors slammed. Loud voices, laughter, running steps moved under us into the hotel. Perhaps I recognized one of the voices, its silky mocking tones. In a few seconds it had died away.

I looked across at Lawrence. 'No,' I said. Through the silvery light I could see he was trying to smile at me. He began to speak again, slowly, with care:

'It was real, you know, what you did, trying to kill me. You mustn't forget that. When I followed you round that's when I discovered what you were like. I wanted to see. It was ironic; I felt for you. At last you wanted people so much and you had put yourself in a position where it was impossible. I wanted to come to you so much, but I didn't.' He turned his head away and his body seemed to sigh. 'Remember that. I didn't come to you. Remember that. When you don't think of me any more.'

We sat across from each other at the breakfast table. The dining-room was as tall and wide and light as a conservatory. Our feet rested against each other under the table. But our hands were busily tapping and spooning at our lightly boiled eggs. And Lawrence still talked. He was making arrangements now and his tone was matter of fact, conversational, almost clipped. He was saying:

'I booked us back on different planes. Don't think of the obvious reason. It's true my wife will meet me now, but I only told her after I decided not to fly back with you. I thought it was better to finish here. Like this.'

His case stood bound and gagged in the hallway. Mine was still upstairs, thrown open on my bed with my belongings scattered liberally across the room.

'I'll leave first. You know, it's strange watching your face now. It seems to be coming into shape while before it changed from moment to moment. The last hours of a sleepwalker. I thought of telegraphing your friends or your family to come and fetch you. But then I thought you would rather finish this alone. Wouldn't you?'

He stopped abruptly as if losing the thread of what he wanted to say and then, continuing suddenly all in a rush, he cried with a warmth of emotion: 'My darling!' It had been happening slowly all the time he had been talking, but now all at once I saw the process speed itself up.

'Yes,' I said, gasping at what was happening in front of my eyes. My stomach wanted to laugh as if I sat in a car going over a hump-backed bridge or in an aeroplane

239

dropping into an air-pocket. I held on to the sides of my chair.

The white morning light was spreading inexorably through the room's tall curved windows. It passed through the huge panes of glass in a million knife-like rays. It filled the room like water in a vase. It drowned sound; it blurred vision. It came to our table where Lawrence was talking and took him out of my sight.

'Oh! Oh!' I cried, unable to contain myself any longer. 'I'm so happy!' And the tears of release flowed down my cheeks and ran into the edge of the pink tablecloth which now I had all to myself.